Harbour Lights

Ian Searle

First published in the United Kingdom in 2023 by

The Cloister House Press

ISBN 978-1-913460-60-0

To

Margaret

Tamsyn

Maggie

For their encouragement and practical help

Chapter one

When I look back over those first two or three years, I conclude that I was amazingly naïve. I was, after all, 32 years old. However, I had spent 17 years of my life so preoccupied with learning my trade that I had ignored almost everything else. That, at least, is how I now excuse my rash decision.

"Mr Hammond!" Jenny at Reception was waving a telephone at me. "It's your father."

I took the receiver from her. "What's the trouble?" I asked. I could think of no reason for my father to call me other than a medical emergency affecting my mother. He and I had never been close. I had left school at fifteen, determined to follow a career in hotels. I was not especially interested in catering, but I loved the idea of owning my own hotel one day. From the beginning I thoroughly enjoyed the work. I had now progressed through all the many different parts of the profession and was Manager of this fifteen-bedroomed hotel, the Pilgrim's Rest. My father was a self-made businessman, a member of a syndicate which he had helped to found many years previously. He, too, had been so bound up in his career that he took little notice of his family. He did not even have my mobile number.

"Hello, Tom," he said, "there's nothing wrong, nothing at all. Can you make yourself free for the day tomorrow?"

"Make myself free? For the entire day?"

"You are the manager. Find somebody else to look after the place for a day."

"I'm not sure – what's this all about?"

"I'll tell you that tomorrow. Find one of your staff to take over the place. What's it called? The Pig and Whistle?"

"It's the Pilgrim's Rest."

"Well, delegate. That's what managers do."

He had a point. I was not good at delegating. "I imagine this is important?" I asked.

"I think so or I wouldn't be wasting my time. This could be good for both of us."

I rang him back half an hour later, and he arranged to pick me up at 7.30 the next morning. He would not say where we were going.

One of the few things we had in common was a love of cars. My father drove a powerful Mercedes. I had scraped together enough money over the years to buy a second-hand Lotus. We were to use neither car. My father arrived in my mother's modest, family saloon. He preferred, he said, to be inconspicuous today. He was casually dressed as was I for once, glad to leave the suit I wore most days. I climbed in with him and we set off. We had little to say to one another.

We drove for nearly three hours, stopping briefly for a snack breakfast. By mid-morning we were leaving the A12 and heading for the Essex coast. This was new territory for me, not, it seemed, for my father. Just before 11 o'clock we arrived at the little town of Goosemere, not quite on the coast, but less than half a mile upstream on the Gann Estuary. We left the car in a small car park. I followed my father as he led me into the principal street, lined with solicitors' offices, antique dealers, small shops, a quiet pub and a small, public library. We arrived at an estate agents' and went in. There were just two small desks. A bearded man behind one of them looked up and greeted us.

"Mr Hammond? We were expecting you. You want to look over the old pub," he said. "I'll grab my jacket and the keys and drive down the hill with you."

"No. I know the way," my father said," we'd rather look round on our own."

It was a firm statement. The man with the beard was surprised but handed over the keys with a warning that some of the timber floors and staircases were potentially dangerous. He was clearly not happy with the arrangement but hoped to make a sale.

We left the office and walked down the sloping street towards the river. I still had no idea why my father had insisted that I accompany him on what seemed to be a routine business trip. At the bottom of the hill the road forked. On the right the road narrowed and ran alongside the river. The tide was out, exposing quantities of black mud. Here and there, small boats sat on this mud. A few yards along, there was a large, stone building on the right, set back a few feet from the road. It appeared to be dilapidated. The building was three stories high, and the many windows were boarded up. Rain, wind, and salt had discoloured the stone. To my surprise this was the building my father was coming to inspect.

"The main entrance is round this way," he said, leading the way into a cobbled courtyard. I wondered how he knew his way round so well. He had obviously been here before.

The great, gloomy building loomed on our left. The boarded-up windows gave it a slightly sinister air. Here in the courtyard it now became obvious how extensive the property was. The main building occupied the entire east side, but in front of us and to our right, on the south and west sides, there were more buildings, similarly run down.

Without speaking, my father led the way into the main entrance. Enough light followed us through the door and came through cracks in the planks to give only a basic idea. The room we were in was a big, low-ceilinged bar. It was filthy. At the north end of this big room, after picking our way gingerly over uneven flagstones, we came to a staircase. Ignoring the warning we had been given, we climbed the stairs. There was a corridor running the length of the building, giving access to seven rooms, empty of furniture. A bathroom and toilet in the middle was unspeakably awful. The plumbing was of lead piping. The wiring was also in need of total replacement and looked lethal. The top floor was a replica of the first. My father said nothing as we inspected this ruin, though he grunted once or twice.

I was relieved to emerge into the courtyard again, but my relief was short-lived. We spent a further thirty minutes exploring the other buildings. Two of them must have been used for storage of some kind. Inside they were like barns.

The inspection over, we headed back to the road.

"What do you think?" he asked.

"I can't believe you would seriously consider buying this place," I said. "Even if you bulldozed the lot and rebuilt, the town is too small to make an investment of that size pay. Houses and flats, next to a stretch of mud wouldn't appeal to many."

"We'll take the keys back and head off for some lunch - not here, there's a nice, country pub a few miles away. We can sit outside and not be overheard."

I was puzzled by his need for privacy.

We walked back the way we had come and returned the keys before driving to the pub in question.

"Well," he said, as we sat with our drinks in the welcome, dappled shade of an apple tree "what do you think?"

"About what in particular?"

"About the Harbour Lights."

"Is that what it was called?"

"Yes, didn't you see the old inn-sign leaning against the wall."?

"I've got a whole list of questions."

"Go ahead."

"To begin with, why on earth would you be interested in such a ruin? I don't know what the asking price is- "

"Offers in the region of 200K."

"It would cost three or four times that to knock it down, and no one in his right mind would want to invest in that little town. It's attractive in its way, but it must have been in decline for half a century."

"What else?"

"Other questions? Well, why did you want me to come with you? You know so much more than me about property, I imagine."

He nodded agreement. "Anything else?"

"It's pretty obvious you know your way around here," I said. "I didn't know anything about that, but then, we've not really had a lot to do with one another for years."

"Right," he said. "You probably never knew I grew up here. In fact, this is where I stole the money to buy my first property."

I stared open-mouthed. It's not every day you learn your father is a thief.

"Don't look so shocked," he said, "it was a long time ago. I was sixteen years old, and, after all, no one got hurt."

I was still staring at him in amazement.

"It was over half a century ago!" he insisted, as though that would make a difference. "I really don't understand why you're so shocked. You know, you've become a middle- aged prude, like one of those fat, complacent ladies you have as customers. Look, I was sixteen. I was living in a dump of a town with parents that didn't care about me. It began as a lark. There was this old man, a bit of a recluse, and it was rumoured he had pots of money. I went to snoop one evening. I was in his garden, peering through the window. I was in the dark. He was sitting in the front room, snoring, in front of a table full of empty bottles. He had obviously been drinking. I found the back door unlocked and half ajar, so I went in – very quietly, of course. I could hear him snoring from there. I don't know what I was looking for – anything I could pinch, I suppose. I got to the foot of the stairs, but I didn't want to risk him waking up while I was upstairs. Then I noticed that some of the treads of the old staircase, which was covered by threadbare carpet, seemed to be bulging. I pulled the carpet to one side and only just managed not to shout out. The old man kept his cash under the carpet! I pulled some of the notes out and stuffed them in my pockets. There seemed to be a lot of them. I had no way of carrying them except in my trouser pockets which I stuffed full, then I made my way out in the dark. The old man was still snoring. I took the money to a little hideaway I had, an old hut, and I counted them – two hundred and thirty-five pounds, all in notes. I put them in an old biscuit tin and hid it. I had enough sense not to spend the money immediately. The old man died the following year."

"Didn't he report it?"

"No, he can't have done."

"He died, you say? What about his relatives?"

"He had no family at all, it seems."

"Didn't any of this come out at the inquest?"

"You are asking a lot of questions about this I had virtually forgotten about it you know. I don't think I have ever told anybody the story in over fifty years. By the way, don't tell your mother. There is no need for her to know."

It was his lack of remorse that shocked me most. He had built a future, it seemed, on a lie at least, a crime certainly.

"Your mother thinks I save the money from the wages I earned working for a local builder. Fat chance of that! I did nothing with it for two years, then I went to a bank in Colchester and opened an account. Nobody asked me about the money. Six months later I bought an old, farm cottage – you could, in those days. I did it up. I made a hundred pounds profit on that sale. I was proud of it."

I was thinking about the original crime.

"Wasn't there an investigation into the missing money?"

"No. The old man probably didn't even notice. I only took half of it, that was as much as I can get in my pockets."

"I can't believe it! That was a lot of money in those days."

"Yes, it was. But either he did not notice, or he did not care. In fact, he died about a year later."

"And it never came up?"

"No. I told you no one got hurt. I wasn't the only one that did well out of it. Whoever it was that cleared out the house and found the rest of the cash, they did quite well. I shouldn't be surprised if the police did not have a good Christmas that year."

I stared at him again in disbelief. He showed absolutely no sign of contrition. It was almost as though having got away with it absolved him of any shame. We were silent for a while and a young waitress brought us the food we had ordered at the bar. It was very good food, but I did not have much of an appetite.

We were sipping our coffee when he surprised me further.

"Right, to business!" he said. "You've been wondering why I wanted you to come with me today."

"If it was to tell me that you are a thief," I said, "it seems a lot of trouble to go to."

"Oh, can we forget about that please? This is important. I have a proposition to put to you, something which I think will be good for you and good for me. I am able to buy the old pub outright. I know I can knock the price down even further."

"Are you serious?"

"Yes. Hear me out. I've been in the development business all my life. To be successful you need three things. The first seems obvious, you need enough capital. The second, maybe not so obvious, is even more important. You need to do your research. Information is worth a great deal in this business. Now, I have many friends and acquaintances, some here in Essex. I happen to know that the county council is just about to publish a new county plan. Part of that plan involves extending Goosemere by building two hundred new houses. The buyers – they will all be for sale – will need additional facilities, like a new school, probably several retail outlets, and various social amenities. If we could do up the old pub and turn it into a truly attractive place, possibly develop a good quality restaurant business, refurbish those dirty old rooms we looked at, we could be onto a winner."

"Well, good luck with that!" I said. "Is this the kind of development your company specialises in?"

"It could well be. That's not what I'm proposing. I said this could be a good thing for you and me."

"There's no way I could invest in this pile of old stones," I said. "I have a little money of my own put aside, but the last thing I would want to do is invest in this."

"What if you did not have to invest personally?"

"I don't understand. In any case I am perfectly happy with the job I have."

"Managing someone else's hotel?"

"I'm doing very well," I said. "It has taken me seventeen years to get to this stage, but Charterhouse is a big company. I reckon within the next ten to fifteen years I could be in line for one of the big, London hotels."

"But you won't ever own it."

"There aren't many big, family-run hotels these days, you know that as well as I do."

"The Harbour Lights could be an exception."

"What are you suggesting that I come and work for you instead of Charterhouse?"

"No. Try listening instead of interrupting. I said there were three things you need to be an entrepreneur in this business. The first was capital, the second good intelligence, the third is vision."

I held my tongue. He was talking earnestly but with the assurance of someone with many years' experience in the financial world.

"I have already suggested," he said," that, with the expansion of the town in the next few years, there will be an increase in demand. If I buy The Harbour Lights for a song and if, between us, we can thrash out a convincing business plan, it could become profitable within, say, 4 to 5 years."

"Why on earth would I give up a perfectly good career which I enjoy to help you start yet another business?"

"I have the contacts and the experience. I also have a vision of sorts. You could provide a fuller, more practical vision. We are ahead of the game now, no one: so far as I know, has yet seen the possibilities. If we seize the opportunity, in a very short time – well, just a few years – we could be running a very successful business here."

"I have said I am very happy where I am."

"But, if you go along with my idea, you could end up owning a modest-sized hotel. I know the place is a filthy shambles now, and it certainly would need a lot of updating – rewiring throughout, re-plumbing, doors and windows replaced, complete refurbishing inside, but, once that's done, there is so much space, and the buildings are structurally sound, that we could have a business running within a year. Within five years it should certainly be making a profit."

"Well, I wish you well with it."

"I have not made myself clear, it seems. I don't want to purchase the place for Hammond and Cartland. That could be Plan B, of course. My partners know nothing of this trip, one of the reasons I wanted to be inconspicuous. I'm sure I could easily convince them to invest. That is not the plan, however. If you agree, I will acquire the property myself as a personal transaction, I will pay the basic price and then give you the deeds as a gift."

"You mean, you would expect me to give up a perfectly good career!"

"Tom," he sighed, "I really thought you had more intelligence. Of course, there is a lot of work to be done. Of course, it will cost a lot of money, money which you don't have – yet. You don't have much by way of security to offer, either. On the other hand, I have been working in this business for a long time and my credit is good. With me as guarantor, we can negotiate a sizeable loan. I am sure I could get the money from the Cornblend Bank."

"It would require an enormous loan, and you can guess my question."

"What's in it for me, you mean? Of course, there must be something in it for me. The kind of agreement I have in mind is that the loan for, say, 400K, will be in your name, repayable over 20 years. For my part, I shall expect a return of 2% of your turnover, to begin once you are in credit, for as long as I, and your mother live. It will be another pension. I don't know how much longer I want to go on before I retire from Hammond and Cartland. It could be ten years it could be twenty, but a little extra income is always welcome."

It was all a very unexpected day out. The proposition sounded at best doubtful, especially since it came on top of the confession. My father's original crime may well have been fifty years in the past, but its revelation involved a total reassessment of our relationship. We had, as I have already said, never been close. Indeed, the family could not be described that way. Nevertheless, this man was my father. He had just told me something he said had been a secret since before I was born, a secret he had not even confided to his wife.

My brain was suffering from overload and emotionally I was exhausted.

"I've already had two pints," he said, tossing me the car keys. "You can drive us back. I've already got six points on my licence, and I could do with another pint before we go. We'll need to go quite early so that your mother can take you back to your Pig and Whistle and get her car back."

"One last thing," he added. "I told you that the new Council Plan is due out in the next day or two: we shall need to move very quickly. I'll need a decision from you within five days."

That, I thought, would be simple. I did not want to take up the offer. The Charterhouse Company, which owned the Pilgrims Rest, had always treated me fairly. I had been with them nearly ten years now. Hotel management is a demanding profession. The hours are long and unsociable, leaving little time for personal interests. That suited me well. I was probably an extremely dull person with few outside interests, as my father had stated. I was single-minded. I was, in consequence, good at my work, and well regarded by my employers. Until my father's proposal, my future was clearly planned. I would continue with the company, moving slowly and deliberately to bigger and bigger hotels in the chain. (The company owned twenty-three hotels, ranging in size from ten bedrooms to a massive sixty-five.).

I drove home. My father dozed much of the time, once he rang ahead and warned my mother to expect us for an early supper. She was delighted to see me, put down my quiet mood to fatigue after a long day, and relished driving me back to the Pilgrim's Rest. I told her about the trip, but said nothing about the surprise confession, nor about the business proposition.

After my return, I went to bed at midnight, first half-heartedly to reports of the day from everyone else. I went to bed but got no sleep at all. I got up at six o'clock, grabbed a cup of coffee, told the startled Robert on Reception that I was going out for an hour or two and I was on no account to be contacted until I returned.

I walked away from the hotel and entered the little wood. A short distance inside, I came to the small river. At the side of a small pond, I arranged myself on a fallen log, enjoying the silence, which was broken only by the sound of water and a few birds. I had stopped here because I knew this was the favourite fishing pond for a kingfisher. Kingfishers are shy birds. I sat without moving, making no sound. All at once there was a flash of brilliant blue and there he was, balanced on his favourite twig. I watched him. His beady black eye was watching the water beneath. Then, in a flash he dived and in a matter of seconds he was flying back to his perch with a small fish wriggling in his beak. The bird threw back his head and juggled with the silvery shape until it was head down, then he swallowed it. It was a privilege to watch. Perhaps it was because I was short of sleep, but a strange thought crossed my mind: I imagine myself as that fish, blissfully unaware of any danger until I had been snapped up and swallowed whole.

I went back to the hotel, ate a little breakfast, changed into respectable clothes, and began the routine of the day. My mind was not on the job. I could not concentrate, a fact which irritated me, making me bad-tempered in my dealings with the staff. That was so unusual they could hardly ignore it. By lunchtime it had dawned on me that my best bet was to let everyone get on with his or her own work

21

while I picked up a bundle of invoices and retired with my computer. Privately, I was cursing my father. He had shattered my peace of mind. Although I had told myself, the moment I had heard his proposition that I could not even think of it, he had managed to press the necessary buttons to leave me feeling very unsettled. He had several times commented on what he called my prudish outlook, he had even compared me to the middle- aged matrons who, I had to admit, made up many my clients. His references to the Pilgrim's Rest as The Pig and Whistle had been deliberately provocative, implying that the job I was doing was of little importance and equated to running a small pub. All of this was irritating, but his cleverest move had been to identify my lifelong ambition to own my own hotel. If I stuck to my present career path, I would never reach that goal. I thought I had fully accepted that until my father had dangled the bait before me, like the silver fish the kingfisher had snapped up.

He did not contact me for forty-eight hours. Two days after our trip to Goosemere I was at the reception desk to allow Jenny an half-hour break. A courier arrived with a parcel addressed to me. I signed for it and opened the flat cardboard box carefully. I folded the box into a manageable shape and put it aside for recycling. It contained a laptop computer. An envelope was sellotaped to the lid and addressed to me. Inside, I found a note from my father.

"In the interests of security," he wrote," I don't want to use my company computers, nor should you use yours for this business. I explained that time is of the essence. If you log on to this machine, (password: harbour), you will find details of how to contact me by email (not my business email, nor even my normal, personal email) or you can contact me, using the mobile number 779654378912."

The irritation I already felt was increased by the cloak and dagger message but, as soon as Jenny returned and had cleared away the paper wrappings and cardboard, I left her to it and retired to my office. I had half a mind to send the damned thing back to him, but he had once more piqued my curiosity which was obviously his intent. There were several programs to look at. I opened the first one. This proved to be another description of his "vision" for the Harbour Lights. There was a slightly more detailed description of the arrangement on which a future contract would be based. The next programme began in Word. It set out the basic development plan in a series of Phases. Each Phase was then roughly costed. Phase One included the clearing of all the rooms in the main building, repairing or replacing damaged windows and doors, repairing the guttering and any missing roof tiles, and re-plumbing and rewiring. This Phase would necessarily involve an extremely expensive operation, using professionals. I thought the estimate for this gigantic task was far too low at £120,000. Phase Two involved the refurbishment of the bar, leading to its opening and the beginning of a revenue source. Labour costs for this Phase could be kept low, if we undertook much of the manual labour ourselves. By "ourselves" he explained he meant myself, himself, and my mother! It might also be possible, he pointed out, to get my brother, Tony, two years younger than me, a teacher, to help in his summer holidays. Much of this Phase would involve such tasks as cleaning, painting, and polishing. Phase Three would eat into the loan further. The plan was to install a decent, professional kitchen, to convert one of the larger spaces into a restaurant, and to begin serving meals. We would need to employ a cook, and the catering business would need to be very carefully costed.

Despite myself, I was intrigued. I was so absorbed in studying all the material in these programs, that I was surprised when Mrs Black tapped on my door and came in with a tray. It was early afternoon. I thanked her, drank the hot coffee, and ate a salad. I was ravenous. I turned off the laptop and, feeling faintly ridiculous, burned my father's handwritten note, tipping the ashes into a metal waste bin. I returned the tray to the kitchen and thanked the chef.

"Don't thank me," he said. "It was young Colin's idea. He noticed you hadn't turned up for lunch."

Colin was a sous-chef, a very promising one, according to Bernard. It was Bernard who told me one day, quoting something he had heard, "Colin is a good sous-chef as sous-chef's go, and as sous-chefs go, one of these days he will. He deserves a kitchen of his own." From Bernard that was high praise.

After reading through all the files twice, I was dismayed and angry to find my resolve was weakening. Risky though the proposition was, if successful, it would enable me to own my own business and, with a little luck and great expertise, it could be free of debt and profitable by the time I was fifty years old. I was in dire need of help and advice. So many years spent moving from one establishment to another to perfect my understanding of the hotel trade meant that I had many colleagues but virtually no friends. I toyed with the idea of asking Tony for his opinion, but he was himself at a crucial point in his career, about to move from his post as Head of Department to the headship of a small, independent school. I contacted two professional colleagues, neither of whom had any direct connection with my present employers. I showed each of them the plans for the Harbour Lights. The solicitor found them unusual but could see no great legal problems. The accountant, John Stanwyck , looked at the spreadsheets.

"It's all a big risk," he said, "and it will depend on whether the town itself becomes prosperous. How realistic do you think the plans are?"

"I can't judge," I said. "All I know is that my father has made a lot of money out of his investments. He told me intelligence was the key and somehow, he seems to have inside knowledge about the County Plan."

"If it works," John said, "you could well make a lot of money. The property alone would increase in value, especially if the town development goes ahead. How much of your own money would you be investing?"

When I told him none, he was very surprised. "Almost an offer you can't refuse", he said. "It's very generous of your father."

He had one change to suggest to Phase One. The income from the bar would not be substantial at first. It would be better to serve food as well. I pointed out we would need a proper, commercial kitchen, something which was planned for later.

"Then why not set up a simple take-away outlet? What about pizzas?"

"Or fish and chips?"

"Good idea."

Without realising it, I was talking as though the decision was already made.

On the fifth day I e-mailed my acceptance, subject to contract. I then made a hasty phone call to the CEO and drove up to town. The die was cast. My contract with Charterhouse tied me to six months' notice. The negotiations with solicitors, accountants, and the bank, together with comparatively simple planning permission (no change of use, but I needed a licence for the bar), took much of this time. My father negotiated contracts to rewire and re-plumb the buildings, including those on the south and west sides. We installed solar panels. My father spent one day each week on site as project manager. For seven months the entire building was surrounded with scaffolding and work was well under way on replacing all the windows – hugely expensive, as the Planning Officer insisted that they should be wooden, not plastic.

Inside, to keep costs down, we got a local builder to modify four bedrooms on the first floor. They became two, double rooms, each with an ensuite bathroom. My father and I undertook the painting of this accommodation so that we could move in. I admired both his energy and enthusiasm but especially his skills, acquired over years but not used recently.

Downstairs we installed a second-hand, domestic kitchen. Eventually, it would be replaced with commercial fittings but for now it would serve our needs. Once that was in place, my mother joined us. She would look after our meals and our laundry. She also picked up a paint brush most days. She had her three cocker spaniels with her and took them on walks in the countryside. She kept them well away from the river; even at high tide it posed a risk, as the dogs, who loved swimming, might end up in the mud.

We worked extremely hard, so much so that I forgot my doubts for days on end. This was such a huge risk for me. At the end of a long day, or on a day of cloud and rain, when the smell of paint hung heavy in the air, I would sometimes pause and allow the doubts to creep in. We spent weeks working in the bar. The old furniture, including the bar itself, was removed and my father set about the joinery himself. It was on rainy day especially, when this low-ceilinged room became a workshop, and the screech of the saw was loud that my spirits sank. It was taking so long, and we were living on borrowed capital. I escaped occasionally, walking along the road by the river, heading away from the town. I would pass the boat park, part of the Sailing Club. Rows of small vessels, shrouded in protective covers, were locked behind the gates, like so many corpses in body bags. Soon after the Sailing Club, a small, wooden hut, was the great, black hull of the Cymbeline, the old, Thames sailing barge. Once or twice the resident owner of this training school waved hello. The road climbed gently and led away from the river, the surface changing to a track. About a mile from the Cymbeline, the track ended at a farm gate. Here I would stop to look back at the river, the solid block of stone that was the Harbour Lights, and the road beyond, rising to the cluster of buildings that made up the town.

At six o'clock one morning, before my parents were awake, I went out to take this walk. As I approached the boat park, in the grey light I saw a woman struggling to unlock the gate. It was unevenly hung and kept swinging close as she tried to open it.

"Can I help?" I asked.

"Thank you," she said. "I've been complaining about this for years. Can you hold it open?"

I did so and helped her uncover a small rowing boat.

"How are you going to get this in the water?" I asked.

"I'll drag it. The tide's in so it's not too bad."

She seemed quite strong, and obviously competent, but it was much easier when I took one end of the boat and carried it to the water.

"If you really want to help, she said, "could you row me as far as my cabin cruiser? It's only a few yards upstream."

"I'm not much of an oarsman," I said, "but I'll risk it if you will."

She laughed at that, a lovely, tinkling, gay sound. The bigger boat, she explained had been stuck on the mud when she sailed back upriver two days ago. She had to wait for the tide to re-float her. She said her name was Elsie and she knew me as Mr Hammond, one of the new owners of the Harbour Lights. Rather clumsily, I took her to the larger boat. It was a few years old, timber built. She went aboard to check if anything had come adrift when the boat, the Moorhen, was lying on her side, then she made the dinghy fast to the stern of the larger vessel, hauled in an anchor, getting smothered in mud. She started the engine which gurgled and snorted into life, and towed me very slowly into a deeper channel. There she made fast to a buoy and re-joined me. I rowed back to the small jetty.

"Thank you …"

"Tom," I said.

"Thank you, Tom. I owe you one. I was going to ask if you liked sailing, but …"she shrugged." One of these days, when we're both free, how about you crew for me and we'll sail down to the sea?"

"That would be interesting, thank you, but I'm not sure about the crewing bit." She laughed again. "I can manage her on my own, but it helps to have someone to make the tea," she said.

We left it at that. She strode off up the hill, her arms still black with mud.

Somehow, weeks passed, and we saw little of one another. Occasionally I caught sight of her at or near the Sailing Club. We waved, but the excursion she had proposed was not discussed until much later. By then, the Harbour Lights project had run into many complications. Meanwhile, we were fully occupied with refurbishments.

This first Phase lasted just over a year. My father's skill as a builder was evident. He listened to all my comments and suggestions, seldom arguing with my demands. One such was the installation of a huge coffee machine at one end of the bar. When my sister, Kitty, four years my junior, took days off from her work in a software firm, where she designed websites, she asked with a grin, "Can it play the Hallelujah Chorus?" I was less certain about the equipment needed for a fish and chip shop. I used it as an excuse to return one day to the Pilgrim's Rest. The staff were pleased to see me. I spoke to the chef and to Colin, explaining what we had planned. I got the technical advice I wanted, but I also told Colin that, once we had a proper kitchen and were ready to begin serving meals, there might be a job for him. He followed me out of the kitchens, however, to suggest he might join us earlier. He was ready to work for bed and board until we opened, he said. I felt a little guilty but accepted. It would, I explained be some time before we could use his skills fully.

Fourteen months after I had taken the fateful decision, we were ready to make a start. We had pulled out all the stops, pushing the necessary authorities, haggled with suppliers to furnish the bar with second-hand, but serviceable, rustic tables and chairs, completed the required inspections, found suppliers. We spent two days posting advertising leaflets through letter boxes. We advertised in the local press and social media, erected a large sign, "Fish and Chips", and set an opening date. We even festooned the courtyard with bunting.

At midnight on the opening night we finished collecting empty glasses but left the debris which littered the yard for an early morning clean-up. We were all exhausted. My parents looked tired, but happy. Tony and Kitty had come to help. Colin, living for the moment in one of our bedrooms which hoped to redecorate within a day or two, brought his machine-made coffee to join us as we tried to take in the success of the first night. For success it had undoubtedly been. The till was bulging.

"I would never have thought so many people wanted fish and chips," said my mother. Perhaps foolishly, she and my father had volunteered to staff the fish and chip shop. Colin had trained them carefully and had popped in from time to time.

"You're going to need more staff," my father said.

"I don't mind helping," said my mother, "but not like that, not every night."

"The bar was pretty busy, too," Kitty agreed, "and Tony and I are only here for a couple of days."

"I know, I know," I said. "Thank you all. I don't think any of us expected so many customers."

"Well, "Colin pointed out, "we knew there was no other fish and chip outlet in the town."

The adrenalin was slowly losing its power. Tomorrow, we agreed, would be a better time to evaluate the evening. Tony and Kitty drove off to the bed-and-breakfast place in town. The rest of us dragged ourselves wearily upstairs to bed.

As usual, I found it difficult to get to sleep. The evening had been a wonderful success, but it had posed new problems, first and foremost, staffing. Recruiting staff would probably be easy but would the budget allow it? I juggled with figures for a long time, got up at 3 am and drank water, stepped outside into the litter-strewn courtyard, sat there in my pyjamas for twenty minutes, and at last went back to bed. The uncertainty which had overshadowed the entire enterprise still dogged me. I could not believe, as the others did, that the opening success would continue.

Chapter two

I can no longer recall the reason that we held our grand opening on a Wednesday evening. All I remember is that it was very successful and that, the following morning, the courtyard was littered with empty packets, the cardboard boxes in which we served fish and chips, and various other detritus. My father and I cleared it up, muttering about the appalling habits of the British public. We swept up the cigarette ends and by 9 o'clock the place looked shipshape again. We planned to open the fish and chip shop the following evening, but my mother looked apprehensive. We needed extra staff. We all got on with our own jobs. Once the bar had been replenished – we had sold a lot of drinks – I took my place behind it with my faithful laptop. Once again, I needed to run the spreadsheets to allow for an extra helper. Since the bar and the fish and chip shop were the only two ways we could generate an income for the foreseeable future, I was very aware that we needed to maximise the income.

I was deeply engrossed in re-calculating the income and expenditure when I heard a voice ask, "are you open for morning coffee?" It was a woman's voice. I looked up apologetically. It was Elsie.

"Elsie! Yes, of course we are. What would you like?"

"A cappuccino, please."

I made her one and passed it across the counter to her.

"You look exceedingly busy," she said.

I explained.

"Yes, I fully understand," she said. "It brings back memories of when I was starting out just a year or two ago. It's a worrying time."

"But you are established now, I take it."

"Yes, but I've had to adapt. I hoped to spend my days making pots and selling them in the shop. I've had to adjust. I now make a lot of my sales online or at local craft fairs. By local I mean anything up to 50 miles away."

"My problem," I explained, "is that I shall have to employ someone to help in the shop. It's not only a question of paying the wages, there's also a problem of finding someone. One young woman last night did ask if there was any work going. I took her name. I must give her a call."

"It's none of my business," Elsie said, "but who is she? I've lived here all my life, so I know most people."

"Her name was Barbara something. I'll have to find a piece of paper."

"Not Barbara Fontwell?"

"Yes, that's it."

"Forgive me," she said, "I can't help being nosy, but I'm not sure I would want to employ Barbara."

"Oh? Why not?"

She hesitated before answering, "let's say I find her a bit unreliable."

"Oh dear!" I said, "so it's back to the drawing board!"

"If it's any help," she said, "a lot of the girls I grew up with still live here and a lot of them are married – a fate I managed to avoid so far. I can think of two or three who would probably be grateful for the chance to earn a little pocket money in the evening."

"I can't just ring them up!"

"No, but I can text them to see if they'd be interested and, if they are, you could talk to them."

She already had her mobile open and began texting. I gave her another coffee on the house. Almost immediately her phone pinged. "Doris is interested, anyway," she said. The phone pinged again. "Oh! And so is Maria. They both said it would be okay for you to ring them." She slid off her barstool and came round to my side of the counter to give me the numbers. We were standing close together and I was looking at her strong, potter's fingers. Neither of us noticed two customers come into the bar.

"Louise!" One of them said, "shop not going so well? Got yourself another job?"

"No," she replied, smiling at the middle-aged man. "Just helping our new friend here. Are you after coffees?"

"Well, it was your idea, wasn't it? You suggested that a decent cup of coffee instead of that instant stuff we have in the hut would be a good idea."

"What would you like?" She was taking over the bar, it seemed.

"Brian would like a cappuccino, so he says. I'll stick to a plain coffee with milk."

"An Americano, then." To my surprise she left me dialling the numbers on my phone and slipped round behind me to the coffee machine where she made the drinks and handed them over. By then I was talking to Doris. She and Maria both agreed to come to see me in the afternoon. Meanwhile, Elsie or Louise had taken some money and put it in the till.

"Thank you," I said. "You seem to know your way around my lovely, new machine here."

She laughed, that tinkering laugh which I liked. "I worked my way through Uni," she said, "as a barmaid. There are times when I quite miss it."

"Louise?" I was puzzled.

Again, she laughed. "My Christian names," she said, "are Louise Charlotte. There were two of us in the same class called Louise. The teacher decided to call me by my initials LC. It's stuck, so all my contemporaries know me as Elsie, but the older people here still call me Louise."

"In that case, I'd be better call you Elsie. I don't want to be classified as the older generation yet."

"By the way," she said, "you haven't listed the coffees on your bar list, so I have no idea what to charge. I charged them two-fifty each. I hope that's okay."

It was very much okay, especially since the first two customers were quickly followed by more, all of them members of the Sailing Club. Elsie had created a clientele for me as well as providing expert service as an assistant. I was to get used to her excusing herself with 'it's none of my business'. She could be as nosy she liked if she was also going to be so helpful.

I liked both her friends and decided to employ each of them for two evenings a week. It was taking a chance that sales would be high enough to cover the additional cost.

There were fewer customers on Friday evening, something we had expected. The opening night had been exceptional. Nevertheless, trade was good, Doris completed her first shift and to the delight of both my mother and Colin, she had worked in a fish and chip shop before, reducing the need for instructions. My mother was especially pleased because she could spend more time away from the fryers themselves, dealing with the money. She closed up and handed me the takings together with the till roll. I closed the bar at 11 o'clock and cashed up. The evening had been a success, but I had a strange foreboding that all was not well. From the beginning of this venture, I had a degree of uncertainty and unease. I was conscious that I had undertaken a very large loan which I could only hope to repay over many years if the Harbour Lights was to become a successful business. That would not be clear for several years yet.

Saturday morning dawned overcast. As we had done the day before, my father and I armed ourselves with large plastic bags and litter pickers and began to clear up the yard. We started at opposite sides, so, although I heard my father's mobile ring, I could hear nothing of his conversation. It was very brief. He closed his phone and put it in his pocket. He dropped the plastic bag of rubbish and the grabber and headed briskly for the door, calling over his shoulder, "Got to go."

I finished clearing up and, 10 minutes later, went back indoors as my father came down the stairs, carrying his laptop and an overnight bag.

"Sorry, Tom," he said, "A bit of trouble at the office, I must go and sort it out. I may have to stay in town for a day or two."

"What about your partners?" I asked, "Why don't you delegate? That's what you tell me to do!"

He was not amused, gave me a sour look, and strode out to his parked Mercedes, jumped in and was quickly off.

"What's all that about?" I asked my mother, who had followed him downstairs.

She shrugged, "it's no good asking me," she said. "You know I never know what's going on in the business. He just does not want to talk about it, not that I would understand it anyway. He just tells me anything that seems to be of importance to me personally. I don't know why, but two years ago now he insisted on putting the house in my name rather than in his."

"That's good, I suppose."

"Is it? He had willed it to me anyway. I don't know why he thought I couldn't wait."

We both went about our business. My phone rang. It was John Stanwyck. "I imagine you've heard the news," he said.

"What news?"

"About Hammond and Cartland."

"What about them?"

"Is your father there?"

"He left about 15 minutes ago. Something about a crisis at the office."

"That is one way of putting it," John said. He sounded grim. "Hammond and Cartland are under investigation. The police raided their offices at 5 AM and are busy collecting all kinds of stuff, computers, files, papers of all kinds."

"My God! What's it all about?"

"I don't know. Usually, when the police swooped like this, they issue a bland statement about financial irregularities."

"No wonder my father drove off like a bat out of hell."

"I will try to find out what I can," said John, "but I think it might be a good idea for me to drive down to help you sort things out."

"Me? What has this got to do with me?"

"I don't know. I'd rather be sure, though. I can be there mid- morning. Have a coffee ready."

He left me thoroughly rattled. I kept myself as busy as I could, avoided my mother, not wanting to alarm her unnecessarily. The uncertainty and anxiety which had been lingering at the back of my mind for so long reawakened. Fortunately, they were not very many customers. My mother went out with her dogs for one of her regular, long walks. I hoped she would not be back before John arrived.

He drove up at about 11 o'clock. He had made remarkable time.

"Can we go somewhere private?" he asked.

I made us both a cup of coffee and we took it into the kitchen. Colin was left in charge of the bar.

"What is all this about?" I asked again.

"I don't know, but when the fraud squad get involved..."

"The fraud squad!"

"That's what they're known as of course. This is something very big, that's all I know. The police are not only investigating Hammond and Cartland, they raided the Cornblend Bank."

"But my loan?"

John nodded. "Exactly. All activities are usually suspended in these circumstances. I am concerned with any involvement you may have."

"Involvement in what, exactly. Except for the loan, I have nothing to do with Cornblend.."

"What about Hammond and Cartland?"

"I have nothing to do with them, either."

"I think you had better tell me all you know about the purchase of this property and how it is funded. As I understood it, your father was going to buy it and handed over to you."

"Yes, that's exactly what he did."

"Was this in the name of Hammond and Cartland?"

I explained that my father had bought the ramshackle property with his own money and had made an outright, official gift to me. It had nothing to do with Hammond and Cartland.

"That is the first bit of good news," he said. "I'm afraid the bad news, the really bad news is that there is a distinct possibility – no, probability – that the bank will foreclose on the loan. Have you any money of your own invested?"

"No, none. It was an outright gift as I said. The loan is essential, because the business is not forecast to be in profit for at least four or five years. That's why it's such a big loan."

"Do you have any capital of your own to keep you going?"

I explained. I had a private account in a merchant bank. The sale of the Lotus had boosted those funds, but they would soon be exhausted. The gravity of it now hit me.

"This could mean I'm facing ruin , I said. "Could I possibly approach another bank and use them to settle the outstanding debt with Cornblend?"

He shook his head. "No bank would touch them with a barge pole," he said. "The FCA, who will have instigated this investigation, only do so when they are pretty sure there is some hanky-panky going on. No other institution was to be contaminated."

"What the hell am I going to do?"

"I can't tell you what to do yet. Try not to panic. It's your father who's in real trouble. If he is mixed up in any of this, he could even end up in court, maybe even jail. Whatever happens, I'll hang around and help as much as I can. I suggest you also alert your solicitor."

By now I was experiencing the physical symptoms of shock. John went next door and got Colin to pour a glass of brandy for me. I have never felt so terrified. I swallowed the brandy and walked out into the courtyard, beating my arms against my sides in frustration. I needed fresh air and I walked blindly to the far side of the courtyard. At that moment I heard my mother calling the dogs to order as she ushered them into the bar. She had not seen me.

John was magnificent. He greeted her, "hello, Mrs Hammond, I don't know if you remember me. I'm Tom's accountant. I love your dogs. There are gorgeous."

Nothing was more guaranteed to gain credit with my mother than to praise her dogs. John chatted amiably to her, giving me time to recover the little. Colin, who had seen me walk blindly out, must have been wondering what this was all about. I did not tell him. I needed time to take in the immense danger I was in, danger of a complete financial wipe-out.

John pretended he wanted to see the fish and chip shop, saying he understood it was doing well. My mother asked him to stay for lunch. He refused gracefully, he had to get back to town, he said.

I asked Colin if he could manage on his own for a while. I needed to make a few phone calls. In my own room I tried to phone my father. His mobile phone was switched off. I rang the company office, or tried to, only to get a 'discontinued' signal. I tried my father's phone several times, each time with the same result. I was already panicking. I checked Hammond and Cartland's website, but it had disappeared. The Cornblend website had also been removed, except for a notice which appeared on the screen. It stated that, due to circumstances beyond their control, they were obliged to discontinue all activities until further notice. In the interest of security and confidentiality the bank would be contacting all its clients by Royal Mail Recorded Delivery soon. I had been abandoned. It occurred to me that my father, for some reason, had been instructed or compelled to cut off his phone. I remembered the laptop which he had sent to me at the Pilgrims Rest. At the time I had thought his cloak and dagger methods were faintly ridiculous. Now I was less sure. I found the laptop and tried the email address. It had been discontinued. I tried the telephone number which he had supplied at the same time. That, too, was discontinued. I was, it seemed, totally alone and in the dark. Only John Stanwyck was trying to help me.

That was the blackest day I had ever experienced. I waited for my father to contact me, but I waited in vain. My panic subsided slightly and began to change into outrage and anger, anger that I had been drawn into this mess by my own father. I had taken him on trust reluctantly. That reluctance was clearly justified. There was nothing I could do. My future, my business, my hopes all rested on decisions made by others. I had no idea what 'financial irregularities' were being investigated. It occurred to me that, in transferring the ownership of the family home to my mother my father had been hedging his bets, putting his assets beyond the reach of creditors, maybe. Was that why he had made me a gift, however small it his eyes, of the Harbour Lights? John Stanwyck had hinted that financial enquiries of this kind were likely to take a long time. I hope that meant I had a little time to come to terms with my predicament. I consulted my solicitor, Roland Simister, half expecting him to walk away from what threatened to be a long and difficult case with little likelihood of ever receiving a fee from me. Fortunately for me, I was wrong.

"I happen to have dabbled in company law," he said. "These cases drag on for years. From what you tell me you may find yourself, let us say, financially embarrassed soon. You may not even be able to pay my fee. However, I am prepared to take it on purely out of interest. Be ready for a very long journey."

There was nothing I could do but wait. I could think of nothing else to do but continue as normally as possible. On Saturday morning Colin took a van to buy some potatoes for the shop that night. He called me on my mobile to tell me that the credit card had been refused. He was obliged to return to collect my debit card for my personal account.

I closed the bar at 2 o'clock and asked Colin and my mother to sit at a table in the deserted room. I broke the news to them.

"I thought something was amiss when the credit card bounced," said Colin. "So, we have a bit of a cash flow problem for a while. How long is it likely to take to sort things out?"

I explained as best as I could. My mother was unwilling to believe how serious the situation was.

"Your father will sort it all out soon," she said. "He's been in business for years. There have been times in the past when I knew something was afoot. He usually told me he needed to work away from home for a bit. He always got it sorted in the end. You just need to hang on and have faith in him." When Colin talked of cash-flow, she pointed out that we were taking money and the shop. She did not appreciate how small the sums were, compared to the outgoings.

Having faith in my father was impossible. Maybe it was as well that she did not fully understand. It was enough that I was inwardly screaming from the stress. Colin, who seem to have a slightly better understanding, showed a similar kind of positive outlook. He did not see the probability that the situation would last for months possibly even for years, long beyond the time when my private funds would run out. He had been so loyal that, even though it was for his own good, I could not tell him to go. I suggested he might start looking for something else, but he insisted on staying, come what may.

The days passed in a blur. Despair dragged me down and away from reality. I hardly slept. There was no news from my father, his company, or the bank. There was still no way of contacting them. Telephone calls to John Stanwyck and Roland Simister brought no clarification. I believe it was this week that the anxiety triumphed and led to the worst, irrational decision of all. I spoke to Colin, who had not only planned a grand, new kitchen, but had also researched the equipment it would need.

"Colin," I said, "if we moved the furniture around in this bar, we could divide it and use one half strictly as a restaurant. I think we could probably get your kitchen up and running within a month. That way we could increase our income. What do you think?"

"Well, of course, I'd love it," he said. "But what about the money. It will cost quite a lot, you realise. Is it wise?"

But my reasoning capability had been destroyed. "It is pretty desperate," I said, "but it would generate a lot more revenue. Could you manage it?"

"Of course, I could, is what I've always wanted. I had already planned the kind of menus I think would work best. It's just the investment in the kitchen equipment."

I was like a suicidal maniac, driving a car towards a cliff. Instead of braking, I was putting my foot hard down on the accelerator. Part of me knew this, but it is astonishing what extreme stress can do.

"OK," I said, "let's do it."

As he had said, Colin had lists of equipment, suppliers, and even electricians ready to fit the equipment. In view of the financial problem, however, he reduced his plans to a less ambitious scale. The first of the fitments arrived within a week, the rest within 10 days. Tradespeople completed the fitting. We had to wait impatiently a further three days for everything to be inspected and approved, but Colin began serving meals three weeks after we had made the decision. Once again, I had to employ waitresses and someone to help Colin in the kitchen. There was no shortage of people willing to take on the work. It was, of course, the sheer madness. The first few evenings were highly successful. Colin's food was excellent, reasonably priced, far better than the usual run-of-the-mill pub food. What I ignored was that this service was unsustainable. Goosemere was too small to support the restaurant. The original plan had allowed for that fact. It had forecast continuing losses for the first four years. It would only be when the population grew that the demand would also increase.

I now believe this was a form of madness, a mania that displaced the enormous anxiety. But it was folly. My world was falling apart, and I knew it.

One morning at this time I was behind the bar with my laptop in front of me. There were only four customers, all from the Sailing Club, one of them was Elsie, another an older man, always referred to as Doc. The postman arrived and asked me to sign for a recorded delivery. I did so. This was the long-promised letter from Cornblend Bank. I realise that my hands were trembling as I found a knife from the cutlery box and split open the envelope. It was what I had been dreading. The bank had not only foreclosed on the loan but was demanding repayment of the money I had so far used. All at once I broke into a sweat and my heart was racing. I could feel it through my T-shirt. I found it hard to breathe. I tried to stand, aiming to rush out into the open air, but my legs would not hold me, and I staggered back to sit on the bar stool. In so doing my hands swept a glass from the counter. It shattered on the floor. The four customers looked round in surprise then, seeing my distress, Elsie and Doc came to my aid. Doc seemed to know what he was doing. He told me to take long deep breaths while Elsie put her strong arm around my shoulders to support me. I thought I was having a heart attack and that I might even die.

"It's a panic attack," said Doc. Later, Elsie told me that he had been a member of the local practice until two years previously.

They called Colin from the kitchen. He told them what everybody knew already that I had been overdoing things of late. When I was feeling a little better, two of them helped me up to my room. I felt quite ill. Elsie knocked on the door a few minutes after I lay down on my bed.

"Doc has pulled a few strings," she said. "You have an appointment at the surgery tomorrow morning at 10 o'clock. I will come and drive you up there."

I protested weakly, but she was adamant. I was told to rest for the rest of the day and avoid any strenuous exercise. Later, my mother looked in and made the obvious comments that I had been overdoing things and should leave more of the work to others. It did not help.

My phone rang. It was Tony. "What's going on?" he asked. "Mum says you had a heart attack."

"No, she's got it wrong again," I said. "It was just a panic attack."

"A panic attacks. That's still quite serious. Since when you have suffered from hypertension?"

"Since I moved into this place," I said. "Look, Tony, you got enough on your plate without worrying about me. I shall be okay. I'm seeing the GP tomorrow."

"I'd be down there like a shot to help if I could. I got my hands full reorganising this place." He was referring to his new school.

"I wish mum had not called you," I said. "There really isn't anything you can do."

"I thought everything was going well," he said.

"It was until this business with Hammond and Cartland."

He knew nothing about it and insisted on being told. He whistled. "This is a real mess," he said.

"Tony, look after your own job. I've got all sorts of people helping me here." It was not entirely true, but I did not want my problems to spread to him.

I had hardly finished speaking to Tony when Kitty called. I tried to tell her what I had told him but, this time, it was with a different result.

"I'm due some annual leave," she said. "I'll drive down and lend a hand for a couple of weeks. You obviously need to step back a bit, take a rest. I can't manage the place for you, but I can help Colin and the others. We can at least ease the load a bit." She was obdurate, promising to be with me by early afternoon the following day. I was beginning to feel that everyone was making too much fuss, that I was even less in control.

The physical symptoms of the panic attack had largely disappeared by the following morning. I felt something of a fraud, taking time up with the GP. If Elsie had not been collecting me, I would probably have cancelled the appointment. On the short trip up the hill to the surgery where, I pointed out, I could easily have walked, Elsie said, "Tom, I'm very sorry, but Colin and I were both very worried yesterday when you collapsed. We guessed it might have something to do with the letter you had received, and you had left it on the counter. We read it, I'm afraid. That's my nosy nature for you. I do apologise."

"Well," I said," we shan't be able to keep these things secret for much longer. It looks as if the Harbour Lights are doomed to be extinguished. I shall be bankrupt."

"There must be something you can do," she said. "I've told you already that I had my own problems when I first started up in business. I thought I was going to go under. I survived, but I had to make changes to my plans. Maybe they were less ambitious than yours, though."

The GP gave me some pills, told me I should take more time off, asked about exercise and diet and asked if there were specific pressures which had caused the stress. My blood pressure, he said, was high. It had probably been much higher when I had the panic attack. His advice seemed ridiculous in the circumstances. There was no way I could take time off or relax. I thanked him, walked the short distance to the pharmacy and collected my pills and allowed Elsie to treat me to a cup of tea in the little tearoom next door. It was strange to be in somebody else's café.

"What whatever else you do," Elsie said, "keep next Saturday completely free. You're coming out with me."

I was about to say I couldn't spare a complete day, then I recalled an identical response I had given to my father over a year ago.

"Where do you want to take me?" I asked, preparing an excuse in my head.

"To the sea," she said. "High tide on Saturday is at 7:05 in the morning. It will mean an early start and we shan't really be able to return until the next full tide in the evening. That's why I say keep the whole day free. I did promise you to take you sailing if you remember. It will be good for you. It's the best way to relax, get away from it all."

I was unsure, but I said yes. Back once more in the High Street, she led me away from the parked van to a small street behind the little hotel. She stopped in front of a shop which, I realised, was where she sold her pottery. Her workshop and kiln were in a room at the back. She unlocked the door and led me in. On the shelves were displayed her tableware, mugs, jugs, cups and saucers, bowls. They were attractive and brightly coloured, not my personal taste, as they were earthenware, rather than porcelain , but I conceded that they would appeal to lovers of handmade goods. She showed me her workshop and the wheel of which she threw her pots. Here, she said, she had fun producing both useful, larger, and bespoke articles, such as vases and a range of figurines. These were sailors in everyday dress, carrying out everyday jobs. They were amusing and very well modelled. These I liked.

I was doing my best not to show that I was impatient to get back to the bar, but Elsie was clearly aware of it and was determined to keep me away as long as possible. It was therefore well after 11 o'clock before we headed down the hill to the Harbour Lights. Colin was there. My mother was walking the dogs as usual. I needn't have hurried back, Colin said. Then he turned to Elsie and said, "I hope you like fish. That's what you got for lunch."

It has not occurred to me that she would stay for lunch, though I was happy for her to do so. Perhaps, I hoped, she would still be there when Kitty arrived. Meanwhile, she chatted amiably to Colin in the kitchen. There was really nothing pressing for me to do. This was not one of the days on which Colin was due to cook and serve meals, so he must have planned this lunch with Elsie beforehand. I checked my emails. There was nothing of importance, nothing from the bank, nothing from my father, nothing from John or from Roland. Elsie re-joined me in the bar and drank an aperitif. My mother returned with the dogs and exchanged small talk with Elsie. I assumed she would join us for lunch. Just before 1 o'clock the only two customers in the bar left, whereupon Elsie walked over to the door and turned the sign to 'Closed'. I was about to protest. This was not her decision to make, but, almost immediately, Kitty arrived. She gave me a hug and asked anxiously if I was all right. Grumpily, I told her I was and that she should not waste her holiday time trying to help me out.

"Oh, don't be such a curmudgeon!" she said. "I like this place. It's got atmosphere, and I like your friends. Hello, Elsie!"

Colin appeared as the two women began to chat. "Lunch in 10 minutes," he said. The two women came to the bar and took the cutlery to lay the table. Kitty called upstairs to my mother to come and join us. Colin served us in person and refused the invitation to join us himself. The food was outstandingly good. Once again, he had used local fish, caught that very night. I was still unsure how Elsie had managed to get herself invited to this family meal, but I was glad to have her there. She was proving a very good and caring friend. Colin served a pudding which tasted excellent, and then joined us for coffee. We congratulated him. The women were doing most of the talking and I was not really listening. Colin was obviously pleased at the reaction to his food.

I was waiting for Elsie to take her leave by about 2 o'clock, the time when the bar would normally have closed and all of us would have two or three hours to ourselves, but she looked as though she intended to stay. I was disappointed in what I saw as insensitive behaviour on her part. I moved away from the table where the three women and Colin were still chatting. They took no notice and I felt curiously excluded. A car drew up outside, the doors slammed, and someone opened the door. It had not been locked. I was about to shout, "We are closed!" when I realised it was John Stanwyck. Roland Simister followed him. John raised a hand in salute and then stopped and looked at the rearranged furniture. "Why the change?" he asked. Colin pointed towards the kitchen. John looked, walked as far as the door, and exclaimed incredulously, "What the hell? What in God's name have you done? How much did this little lot cost?"

Once again, something in me snapped. I was processed by rage. "It's the only way we can make any decent money here," I said all, rather, shouted. I felt as though someone else had taken me over, I found words coming out of my mouth without thought or planning and I was absolutely back against a wall, as though fighting off a snarling dog. "Can none of you stupid people understand?" I shouted. "We have finished, finished! To hell with the lot of you!" I strode past the two men who stood, astonished as I left the bar and slammed the door behind me. In the courtyard I walked rapidly away from the door, kicking a plastic, rubbish bin so hard that I made a hole in its side and sent it flying several yards. I had no idea where I was going except that it had to be away from the Harbour Lights. A little later, slightly out of breath, I was well on the path to my farm gate. My anger began to subside a little, but it was fed by a strong sense of alienation. Elsie, who that morning had seemed to be a good friend, had been very happily engaged in conversation with my mother, my sister, Colin who had fed her, fed all of us and all four showed no sign of understanding how I felt. The two professional advisers who, I had temporarily forgotten were trying to help me with few prospects of being paid, were harshly critical of my decision to install the new kitchen. In my heart of hearts, I knew the decision had been extremely foolish, but John's reaction had confirmed it as fully and taken away any vestige of self - belief.

I reached my gate before I realised that I had been shouting obscenities at the top of my voice. There was no one to hear me fortunately. The cool, empty silence calmed me a little. I had nowhere to go but back to the pub. I realised that my behaviour had been unforgivable and inexplicable. I did not fully understand it myself. With a heavy heart and a growing sense of shame at the prospect of having to apologise, I walked slowly back down the hill. To anyone watching I must have presented a dismal sight of total dejection, like a dog who has been discovered stealing the Sunday lunch.

I squared my shoulders and took a deep breath before opening the door. The six of them were still sitting at the table. They had drinks in front of them. They looked round and Kitty, who was closest to me, got up and ran to meet me. She put her arms round me, just as I was trying to say, "I'm sorry. I don't know what came over me. I'm so sorry." My voice was breaking an uncertain. Kitty took me by the elbow and steered me towards the stairs.

"You need to lie down," she said, and I let her guide me halfway up the stairs. I was weeping. In the privacy of my own bedroom, I sat on the bed and gave way to grief. I had no idea what the group downstairs was doing, nor did I care. I was only grateful that no one disturbed me. I had lost track of the time. At last, I stood under the shower and allowed the water to wash some of the weariness away. And I was immeasurably weary. The last thing I wanted to do was to speak to anybody, but I would have to speak to Kitty and my mother, even if I managed to avoid the others. I went back to the bar, still shaky.

"Tom," John said, "I am so sorry to have upset you. This is neither the time nor even the place to talk. We are all concerned about you and your health. You must take care of yourself. This project may be less important than you think. Your health comes first. Roland and I will be off, but we will be in touch. Don't think we are abandoning you. Far from it."

They both stood up and took their leave. John had given Roland a lift. They said goodbye briefly to the others. Elsie said goodbye briefly with a smile to everyone. She kissed me on the cheek and left the rest of us. My mother gave me an uncertain pat on the arm to comfort me, then made off to her own room. Kitty indicated that she would help Colin clear up the kitchen but, before she did so, Colin presented me with a cup of tea which he put on the table, not the bar. I was being tactfully steered away from work. I gave in. The emotional outburst had been like an eruption of bile. I had a little feeling that except tiredness. I could not even be bothered to speak to anybody. I dragged myself back to bed and lay down.

I was like a zombie for the next two days. I made no decisions, gave no orders, took no part in the day-to-day work of cleaning, restocking, washing-up or manning the bar. Kitty worked quite hard. There was no sign of Elsie. I learned later that she had been busy in her shop and had not liked to "intrude" in the evenings. My mind was almost blank. The nearest they came to normal feelings was with the dogs. I told my mother that I would take them for their walks for the next two days, an offer which surprised her. She was happy for that to happen, however, and, while I could talk to them, I knew they would not ask me any silly questions. There are times when the unquestioning love of the pet is worth a bottle full of medicine. They certainly helped me to heal.

On Friday evening I suddenly remembered I was due to accompany Elsie on her boat in the morning. It would be better, I thought, then hanging about the pub, though I was not sure how Elsie would react to my early morning appearance. Nevertheless, I put on an old pair of jeans, a T-shirt and a sweater and walked as far as the Sailing Club just before 7 o'clock. She had brought enough food, she said, for both of us. There were waterproof jackets as well as life jackets on board the Moorhen if the weather became chilly. I help her load the gear into the dinghy. She rowed this time. We made fast the dinghy to the buoy, started the engine, and began the slow trip down the estuary.

"She's old, and slow, but she's reliable," Elsie said of the Moorhen. "She was built before the war by a local man. He and his wife were both quite large, I'm told, so he deliberately built her broad in the beam. You can see why when you look inside the cabin. There are two bunks, but they are much wider than usual, very comfortable in fact. But being wider, she is slower and need a bit of coaxing under sail. We'd never get to the sea if we had to tack. It is easier to use the engine. You can just sit there and enjoy it."

I was content to do just that. I had never been down the river before, so I watched the scenery, while Elsie steered us from buoy to buoy along the main channel. We passed the point at which the river curved right. The road bridge on the left spanned only a small creek, dry except at high tide. Once it had been navigable, like the rest of the Gann. An old, wooden wharf, now disused marked where the lighters had once brought timbers from vessels of a deeper draught. Then we were in almost featureless country. Saltmarsh stretched on either side. The interest here was largely the wildlife. Elsie, I was glad to note, was happy not to talk. The motor chugged steadily, otherwise the only sound was the light switching noise of water along the sides. We were sailing into the sunrise. After an hour the air was appreciably warmer.

"There's no danger of running aground here," Elsie said. "There's a decent little breeze, enough for this old girl. Give me a hand to get the cover off the main sail."

It took just a minute or two. Following instructions, I managed to raise the foresail and soon Elsie had the Moorhen running before the light, offshore wind. It was even more peaceful without the motor. The tide, now on the ebb, helped us along, but we were in no hurry. We were at the mouth of the estuary now. The boat lifted a little, but it was a calm day. I was secretly quite grateful, not knowing if I was liable to suffer from seasickness.

"Where are we heading?" I asked.

"Nowhere in particular," she said. "I thought we might head a couple of miles up the coast and do a spot of fishing."

"Fishing? We don't have any rods."

She laughed. "Line fishing," she said. "The simplest form of fishing there is. All you need is a line, hook, and bait. I've got some bits of bait in a plastic box. Don't try to eat it yourself."

She was right about sailing being the most relaxing activity. All the cares which had dogged me for the past few days were all but forgotten. The shoreline was not very interesting, being quite low lying and flat. We saw no other boats. When Elsie turned the boat into the wind and dropped the mainsail, it could have been almost anywhere. On her instructions I threw the anchor overboard. There was very little swell, and the Moorhen sat like a large, brown seabird on the water. We had a hot drink, made in the tiny galley area, and ate a sandwich. I felt hungry: the sea air had awakened my appetite. Then, from under one of the seats on which we were sitting in the cockpit, Elsie produced two lines wound carefully round their frames. From a plastic box she produced bits of fish and some crab meat. She loaded it expertly onto the hooks with her strong fingers before handing me one line and dropping the other over the side.

"Now what?" I asked.

"Now we wait for the fish, if there are any."

Nothing happened for a long time. I was beginning to think this was a particularly boring exercise, when I felt a tug on my line. I tugged back and was instantly amazed at the strength of the creature of the other end. Whatever it was, it must be strong. Elsie moved closer telling me to pull it in not too fast, but to keep tension on the line. From some where she produced a net on a handle. At last the fish broke the surface. It looked enormous and I was unsure how to bring it in board, but Elsie manoeuvred the landing net underneath this monster and with a heave of her shoulders, she landed it in the cockpit. It was a cod, over 2 feet long, and it thrashed about on the floorboards until Elsie found a large wooden object with which she struck the poor creature once, hard, and it stopped moving.

"I'm not sure I like having to kill such a lovely thing," I said.

"What you have to remember," she said, "is that this lovely thing has spent all its life so far eating other fish. It's a predator. They will eat anything. We are predators. We are all part of the natural food chain, though, I have to admit, not many human beings get eaten."

We gave up fishing then, stowing the cod somewhere where it could be kept reasonably cool until we went ashore that evening. Colin would make good use of it.

This little bit of excitement changed the atmosphere. The sun had now moved to the south, back the way we had come from the mouth of the river. It was quite warm.

"Nearly time for lunch," Elsie declared, "time for a quick swim first, I think."

"I didn't bring any trunks," I said.

She laughed again. "You don't need trunks out here," she said. "There's no one to see us and, in any case, it's much better skinny-dipping. There's nothing like it."

Before my startled gaze she was already removing her top, then her shorts and her underwear.

"Come on!" she said, completely unconcerned at her nakedness. She stepped up to the transom, threw her arms wide and dived into the water. She took half a dozen, powerful strokes away from the boat, then swam back to tread water, waiting for me to join her. Embarrassed, I too stripped. I could see that she was a far better swimmer than I was. She had strong shoulders and arms. She swam completely round the boat, laughed at my weaker efforts, and seemed as happy in the water as if she were on dry land. As for me, I did not state in very long. The water was quite cool, not to say cold, this was, after all, the southern end of the North Sea. I scrambled back on board, conscious that it was not a very elegant way to get out of the water. Elsie remained where she was for a little longer but, when it was her turn to climb back on board, she swam alongside, and with one, smooth heave, brought herself on board. We sat on opposite sides of the cockpit, dripping water. Elsie was laughing. "I'm afraid there's only one towel," she said. For the first time she realised that I was looking at her naked body. She looked at me and grimaced.

"Have you never done this before?" she asked.

"No."

She laughed then. "Well," she said, "you have lived a sheltered life. You look as though you have never seen a naked woman before."

She was laughing at me. I was not sure whether I was embarrassed or not.

"I don't mind your looking at me," she said. "I'm perfectly happy in my own skin. Are you? There's not much wrong with you that I can see."

This was an extraordinary experience for me. I was not a virgin. I had, indeed, seen other women undressed, but none with the same lack of self-consciousness. Elsie had a strong, mature body. She clearly did not mind my looking at her. She stepped down into the cabin and retrieved the towel.

"I won't dry my hair," she said. "That would be unfair. She stood, now close to me to towel herself down. I don't know if she was deliberately teasing. For all I knew, she might have been seducing me. She did not protest when I stood and kissed her. In fact, she responded warmly.

"Ugh! You are still wet," she said. "Dry yourself off a bit. I want to wash the salt out of my hair. From the cabin she brought a large plastic bottle of fresh water, knelt on the seat to lean overboard, and poured the water over her hair before stretching out

68

an arm for the towel which was already quite wet. She wrapped it around her hair like a turban. In so doing, she raised her hands above her head in a classic, artist's model pose. I suddenly saw she was beautiful and said as much. She thought I was mocking until she looked at my face and saw I was serious.

"I'm not beautiful," she denied. "I'm just ordinary, ordinary and fit."

"No, you really are beautiful," I said.

Neither of us quite understood what was going on. I'm sure that Elsie had not deliberately sought this kind of intimacy. Given my present state of mind, this was a complication I would not have sought for myself, but I was beginning to feel that things were happening to me, that I was not in control of them. Indeed, when I was in control, I seemed to make disastrous decisions. Perhaps it would be as well just to let circumstances control me for once. Reason, I now recognise, had little to do with it. Perhaps it would be best to let other people do the thinking for me.

She was right about the bunks. They were comfortable and wide. We lay together and enjoyed each other's bodies. It was a time out of time. For me it was the beginning of a healing process. I did not know exactly what Elsie was thinking if, indeed, she was thinking at all, but she, like me, seemed lost in the moment. We lost track of the time then, beginning to feel cool, we pulled the sheet over our naked bodies and fell asleep in each other's arms.

Much later, we told each other quietly something of our lives before we met. Elsie told me about her parents, now retired and living in Spain. She was an only child, a happy one. She had attended a primary school in Goosemere, then a Comprehensive school. She was not an especially gifted pupil, she admitted, but she had completed her sixth form work and secured' a place at a university which offered courses in Ceramics and Art. It was exactly what she wanted. At the age of 21, with her parents' backing, she had begun making and selling pots. Now, 10 years later, she had an established business and was very happy. She had many friends, so, when her parents decided to settle in Spain in their retirement, she was quite happy to remain behind.

I told her my own story. I thought it was quite dull, but she was interested in hearing of all the various establishments I had worked and trained in. It was a lazy, murmured conversation. The time slipped by imperceptibly until Elsie exclaimed, "what's the time?" I picked up my watch which I had taken off before we went swimming. It was 4:30.

"Oh my God," she said. "We shall have to get moving. We can't miss the tide. Once it turns, I doubt if we will make it back up the river. It's amazing how fast the current runs."

"What time is high tide?" I asked.

"Roundabout 6:30, but we've got to get down to the estuary, and then it will take us about an hour, even with the tide to help us."

Reality had broken into my dreamlike idyll. I did not want to go back. I could happily have spent the night and even longer in this isolated, wonderful, peaceful world with the woman who cared for me, someone who was generous, giving and to make me feel alive. Now, however, she became the captain of this little vessel. At her command I helped her raise the sails and retrieve the anchor. I half expected it to be covered in mud, but the bottom here was sandy. The land was beginning to cool off, producing an onshore breeze, enough to drive our broad-bottomed boat south. Elsie was at the tiller and kept one eye on the sail above us. I sat and watched her. She was conscious of my gaze, but it did not worry her. From time to time, she took her eyes off the horizon to look at me and smile. She had no regrets, it would seem. I certainly had none. For the first time in weeks, I felt calm. I did not want to face the problems which awaited us, but I was now ready to do so.

At last, we reached the mouth of the river. Elsie warned me to watch out for the boom, then pushed the tiller away from her. The sail fell over to port with a thudding sound, the boat heeled a little in the same direction, and we swung round towards the sun in the west. The wind and the tide now worked together. There was no need for the engine as we sailed slowly upstream. We reached the mooring in the early evening. Between us we furled the sails and tidied the cabin area. We rowed ashore without speaking. A couple of fellow club members shouted hello as we stowed the dinghy in the boat park, then laden with several bags, including a very wet towel and an extremely heavy, canvas bag, containing the fish, we walked down to the Harbour Lights.

"I'm not coming in," Elsie announced. Seeing my disappointment, she explained, "I have a craft fair in Ely tomorrow, and I have to load the van yet."

"When will you be back?" I was unable to conceal the eagerness in my voice.

"I'll get back in the small hours, and I have to open the shop on Tuesday."

"Tuesday evening, then?"

"Sorry, Tom. I must load my kiln on Tuesday and start a firing."

She realised I did not understand the implications. "I have to watch the kiln as the temperature rises and keep it steady. That's an all-night job. It means I shall be busy all week, I'm afraid."

"I'm not sure I can do without you all week," I said clumsily.

She laughed at that, then she put down the bags and kissed me. "It's been a lovely day," she said. "You look so much more relaxed."

I watched her for a while as she walked away, then I turned into the courtyard.

There were one or two early evening drinkers in the bar, served by Kitty. She waved a hand, expecting me to chat, but I was not in the mood. Certainly, the dead weight of anxiety and the sense of waiting for the final disaster had lightened, but the worry still lingered. I was more than a little confused about Elsie's attitude, too. It was almost as if she was using her pottery as an excuse not to see me. Surely, I had not been completely deceived? She had shown deep concern. We had slept together. It had to mean more than a casual fling, didn't it?

I found Colin in the kitchen and presented him with my fish. He was impressed and said he would fillet it immediately. He wanted to ask questions about the day, but he was busy. I got away quickly and went to my room. Under the shower, memories of Elsie's touch, of her fingers on my skin, came together with the pictures of swimming, naked in the sea. I could not bring myself to go back downstairs until much later.

The bar was almost empty by then. Kitty, free for a while, was able to chat. She said I looked more relaxed, that a day at sea had clearly been good for me. Where was Elsie, she asked? I explained about the trip to Ely, but Kitty was giving me a curious look. She sensed there was a story to be discovered. She probably imagined Elsie and I had argued. It would be a while before she discovered how wrong she was. She helped me cash up before we had a goodnight drink, turned off the lights and went to bed.

I lay awake once more, but not to lie worrying about money and lawyers and the future of my business. I was enjoying those magic hours in the small boat. I was almost reluctant to fall asleep.

Chapter three

I woke the next morning to the sound of rain on my window. I swung my legs out of bed and looked out. The tide was not full and it was impossible to tell if it was coming in or out. I looked at my bedside clock. It was 8.30 am. I had slept like a log.

The others had already eaten breakfast. I was about to make myself a coffee when Kitty beat me to it and ordered me to sit down. Colin said breakfast was on the way and brought me eggs Benedict. I was not sure whether I was being treated like a guest or as an invalid. It was Sunday. We would open the door for two hours at lunchtime, then again at six o'clock. If the bar was empty by ten, we would close then. The chip shop was not scheduled to open until Tuesday. This was as close as we came to taking a break, but that, as I knew very well, was what the catering trade was like. My mother was not on duty for the next two days. It was a time we could all relax in theory, except that we were all conscious of the threat that hung over us.

My mother joined me as I drank my third cup of coffee. "You are looking a lot better this morning," she said.

"It must be the sea air," I said.

"Well, whatever it is, you look a lot less stressed. You really shouldn't get so worried, you know. I'm sure this trouble will be sorted out soon. Your father …"

"Dad? He's the one who got me into this mess."

"I was going to say," she continued, "your father rang yesterday."

"You spoke to him?"

"Yes. He told me not to worry, he was all right. They've taken his mobile away for some reason. I didn't think they could do that. He had to phone from a public phone box. I don't even know what they look like anymore. I'd be looking for one of those big, red phone boxes. They seem to have taken them all away now."

She would probably have rambled on for hours.

"Did he have any message for me?"

"For you? No. He said the solicitors were sorting everything out."

I let the subject drop. Kitty joined me as my mother got up. "Well?" Kitty asked.

"Well, what?"

"What happened yesterday?"

"You know what happened. I went out for the day on Elsie's boat. I caught a great big fish. I think Colin plans to make lunch with it."

"That's not what I mean, and you know it."

"What do you mean, then?"

"We don't understand," said Kitty, "why you seem so much more cheerful, but Elsie didn't come in to say hello. Have you two fallen out?"

I had a brief picture of the two of us diving off the boat, and I laughed.

"You can be so infuriating at times!" she said.

"I was just thinking that it's not a good thing to fall out of a boat."

I was not ready to share the memory of that day with Kitty, or anyone. We talked about other things. I got up and left Kitty for a while. "Wait a minute," I said and went to my room. I came back with my laptop.

"Tom," she said, "it's Sunday. Don't waste time looking at spreadsheets."

"I'm not," I said, "shift up."

I moved to sit next to her while I Googled "L.C. Marchant". Elsie's website sprang into life. There was a thumbnail picture of Elsie, a few lines about her and her work and a Gallery. One could order items using online order forms. Kitty liked the tableware, thought she might treat herself and her work colleagues to some mugs. A subsection of the website was entitled 'Studio Pottery'. This showed brightly coloured vases and a few pieces which were simply decorative, never designed to hold water, let alone flowers. We both like some of these pieces. The figurines came last, skilfully modelled, carefully coloured. These were made from a finer sort of clay. Nearly all off then were of sailors or people messing about in boats. They were generally amusing, models of people in mildly awkward situations. One was of an oarsman who had caught a crab. He was falling backwards, clutching the oars as he fell with a look of panic on his face. Another, was of a young woman, painting the bottom of a boat. She was lying on her back and there were smudges of paint on her face and hands and a little puddle of paint on her stomach. A third showed a young man who was being pulled overboard by a fishing line, having caught something far bigger than he expected. In every case the face was finely modelled and painted. If these were inspired by real people, then they would be identifiable.

"A talented lady, your Elsie," Kitty commented.

"She's hardly *my* Elsie," I said. "I've only known her a matter of weeks. She was born and bred here."

Kitty said nothing, but I knew my sister. She was thinking furiously, adding two and two to make five. I had no intention of telling her if she was doing her sums right.

"I didn't know you were a web browser" she said.

"I'm not. I know how to look things up when I need to. I don't have your skills."

"What about Facebook and Twitter and the rest?"

"No, I never look at them. I know social media are useful, and I know they must be your bread and butter, but, if I ever need them, or think they could be useful I'd get someone else to do it for me."

"Get you!" she said, "the social media *are*! Like your use of the plural. Very correct!"

Colin took a break and came to join us while he drank his coffee. As he walked to the table, he saw the lid of the laptop. He frowned, about to say something, but Kitty caught his eye and I thought she shook her head slightly. It felt like a private signal.

During the days that followed, on several occasions, when some of the older 'sailors' were in the bar, on one occasion when my mother and Kitty were talking about the old hut which served as HQ for the Sailing Club, I glimpsed what I thought were conspiratorial nods, winks, nudges, lifted eyebrows, a grimace. I tried to suppress these unreasonable suspicions. I had enough to worry me without conspiracy theories.

Roland Simister phoned. I tensed, anticipating bad news.

"Tom," he said, "I want to be prepared, and I've been talking to John Stanwyck."

"Yes, prepared for what?"

"For every foreseeable demand the bank and your father's solicitors can throw at us. We think it would be a good idea to do a new valuation of the Harbour Lights."

"Why, and what would that involve?"

"John says he'd like to be there, but we will need to get two estate agents who specialise in commercial property to do the valuation. They could be asked to consider the new installations, like the solar panels. I'm sure they will be classified as fittings and fixtures. You have done a lot to the property. Its value may surprise you. It's your father's solicitors who may suggest you sell up. I can't at the moment guess at the others. What I hope is that the two firms will try to fight it out between them, while we deny liability. In a sense, your part in all this is quite minor."

That was not how I felt. My future was at stake. As for being surprised by the proposed valuation, nothing, I said, would surprise me anymore. I agreed to go ahead, and the valuation was arranged just one week later. In the meantime I felt more and more like an outsider in my own pub. Colin and Kitty took over the daily running of the business. They only came to me when I had to pay a bill or approve an order. It felt much like I was working as a manager again, but now I felt uneasy. I was being forced to delegate against my will.

I did not attempt to contact Elsie until Wednesday, by which time I assumed she would have been about to unload the latest pieces from the kiln. I rang her mobile, but it was switched off. I felt an irresistible urge to see her, so I walked up the hill to her pottery. It was in darkness and the Closed sign was on display. I was worried. By now the rosy glow which had been left from our day together was fading. The disappointment I felt as I stood on the narrow pavement in the back street was more intense because it contrasted with our experience in the Moorhen. For a moment I had glimpsed something like joy. Now I was back on my own, hope almost completely overtaken by despair once more. I bought a cup of tea in the café we had used before and tried to gather my wits. I realised I was behaving like a love-sick adolescent. It was a complication too far. I did not know what Elsie was feeling, after all. She was off somewhere, carrying on with her life and might well have forgotten about our day together. Maybe it was just a one -day fling after all. I trudged moodily back to the Harbour Lights, but walked on, past the boat park and the Cymbeline. The Moorhen at her buoy. I walked vigorously until I reached the gate, slightly out of breath. I leaned against the wood and gazed down at the Harbour Lights with the distinctive, solar panels, and at the hill beyond, leading to the town where I had just drunk tea. I felt quite lost and aimless.

When I went back in through the main door, Kitty and Colin were standing close together looking at Kitty's laptop. I thought they sprang apart when they saw me. Surely there was nothing going on between them. I had not noticed any other signs to suggest such a thing. Was this paranoia?

"The post has been," Kitty announced. She handed me a thick letter from my bank, a statement, no doubt. I took it to a nearby table and slit it open. A printed statement showed my payments for the month, the daily takings from the chip shop and the bar. It also recorded withdrawals, which exceeded the deposits, as I expected. I was a little puzzled that I had been sent a print-out, but the covering letter explained. I had not withdrawn more than a few pounds for pocket money for months until Cornblend had stopped my account with them My personal account had suddenly become very active. The letter told me the sudden change looked as though I was now using the account as a business account. It was also apparent that I was spending more than I was depositing. In the circumstances I was invited to an appointment to discuss other, possible arrangements. I might need to set up an overdraft facility, for example.

Kitty was looking at me. "Bad news?" she guessed.

"I'm not sure, but I think so." I could feel my blood pressure rising. I asked her for a glass of water and groped in my pocket for pills the doctor had given me. Kitty watched anxiously as I took myself upstairs. I told her I'd be OK but the pills took a few minutes to work, then I went to my room and called John. He reassured me as much as he could and suggested an overdraft could be a good idea.

The appointment was for the day following that of the valuation visit. "I think it would be best," John said, "if I were to come with you to see your bank manager. I'll draw up a modified business plan. I don't want you dealing with him alone. He doesn't need to know anything about the Cornblend business. Technically speaking, no one has a lien on your property. If we can get you an overdraft, it will certainly buy us more time."

"A lien?"

"A possible claim which would have to be settled before you could take payment from a sale."

After repeated attempts I contacted Elsie that evening.

"Tom," she said, "sorry if you've been trying to speak to me. I'm sorry, but I told you I was going to be busy with the kiln. I still am. And after that I have to drive off again on Saturday. I shan't be around for the next ten days. I'll let you know when I'm back."

"Ten days?"

"I'm afraid so."

Once again, I wondered if my imagination was playing tricks. Her tone was not even that of a warm friend. It was guarded, as though she was hiding something. I pressed the little red telephone symbol on my mobile and sat, staring out of the window. The tide was out, and the sky was grey. My mood was bleak. It occurred to me that, when I had visited her shop earlier, it had been dark inside. If she was tending to her kiln, why would she leave it? Why would she lie to me? Was this yet another betrayal?

I was still sitting there when Kitty knocked on my door and came in. "Oh, Tom!" she said, "you look dreadful again."

She sat next to me, put an arm round me, leaned her head on my shoulder. "It will all be all right," she said. "I know how awful this is for you, but there are some of us trying to help. You'll pull through this in the end."

I was thinking how small and delicate her arms were by contrast with Elsie's. Kitty offered me a gentle, sisterly solace, and I was grateful, but she was not what I needed at that moment.

"Lie down," she said. "I wonder if we can get the doctor to make a home call."

"No, they don't do home calls these days," I said. "I'll be all right in a while. It's the waiting that's the worst thing."

She looked at me as she stood up. She seemed to want to say more, then thought better of it. "I'll bring you a cup of tea," she said. "You should lay off the caffeine."

The days passed. Kitty extended her two weeks to help at the Harbour Lights. She could work at home, she said, thanks to modern technology. Her boss was OK with the arrangement. Trade continued much as before. The profits made on Colin's excellent food were modest, not enough to begin to recoup the expenditure on the equipment. The bar made a little money. The fish and chips made more, but over -all the place was losing money.

John Stanwyck arrived early on the day of the valuation. He accompanied the man and the woman valuers as they looked, first at the occupied wing. They noted everything, including the fittings and the deep fat fryers. Then, accompanied by John, they inspected the south and west wings. These had ben rewired and re-plumbed, and there were solar panels on the roof, but inside the rooms and spaces remained empty and derelict.

I served coffees, hoping they would give me an instant valuation, but they said they needed to return to their office and consult.

"My fault," John explained. "I wanted them to estimate values of the three wings separately as well as together."

"Why?"

"We might be able to tell your bank manager there's sufficient equity in the West wing to secure a bigger overdraft."

"But they haven't worked out the figures."

"They promised to email the rough estimates this evening. It's cutting things a bit fine for tomorrow's visit to the bank, but I've worked up some provisional figures. I might have to burn the midnight oil. With a bit of luck, I may see a way you may even be able to pay my fee." He grinned. I smiled weakly, thinking how generous with his time he had been.

He stayed overnight in the old hotel. ("Old and creaky, but passable,") he said. He drove down to collect me. He would take me to the bank, since I could not drive there in the van, and I would come back by train as far as the nearest station, ten miles from Goosemere. There I would phone Kitty or Colin to collect me. For the first time in weeks, I felt a pang of regret at the loss of the Lotus.

"Did you get the valuations?" I asked, almost as soon as we set off.

"Yes," he said, "and they were better than expected."

"How much?"

"Enough to convince your bank to give you a decent overdraft," he said. "You'll be able to see exactly when we get there."

"But roughly?"

"Be patient, Tom. I'd rather give you the exact figures they gave me. You'll see how I incorporate them in the new business plan. By the way, I'd rather you left all the talking to me. You won't be completely familiar with the plan."

Once more it seemed, other people were in charge. I did not much like the feeling. I fell silent.

"No news of your father, I take it?" he asked.

"He managed to ring my mother from a public phone box just to tell her he was all right. They, whoever 'they' are, have taken his phone away."

This did not surprise him.

I did not want to talk about my father. I sat back and watched as the featureless motorway passes under our wheels. We were running a little late, but we parked with five minutes to spare and when the Manager came out to greet me, I introduced John.

The Manager was not surprised. He asked someone to bring coffee for us.

John took papers from his briefcase and passed copies to me and Mr Coombs. He had prepared an outline business plan. He explained that my father was a professional developer who had bought the old buildings and done some basic restoration before giving them to me as a gift.

"How very generous!" exclaimed Mr Coombs.

"I think," said John, "he was probably trying to offload some assets to ease his tax load. He obviously intended to leave the property to his son eventually. This way they can avoid death duties."

We turned to the business plan. While John continued his remarkably glib description, I was looking down at the papers, hiding my expression. The valuations were astonishing. I realised the renovations and installations to the East wing had made a difference, but the East wing alone was now worth 350K. It would have been far more as a going business had it not been operating at a loss. John suggested things would change within three years, as Goosemere was already starting to grow and there were, he said, plans to develop the riverside. There were also plans to open an Agronomy Research establishment to the southwest. Meanwhile it was suggested we might sell the West wing, with its solar panels, its new wiring and plumbing. This could provide co-lateral for a sizeable overdraft or loan. The West wing was valued at 120K. I struggled hard to conceal my surprise at all this.

We emerged an hour later. John had a smug grin on his face. I had a new cheque book. I could at least treat him to lunch before I boarded a train.

Kitty picked me up. "You look happier," she said.

I told her what we had arranged. "You'll still be in debt for a long time," she remarked, bringing me down to earth.

She was right, but we had at least gained time. On reflection, John's business plan was improbably ambitious. It was unlikely we could turn a decent profit within three years, especially since a major contribution in the original scheme, would come from developing the accommodation. Once you have rooms to let, each occupancy is virtually clear profit. All it requires is staff to service the rooms. Guests would want to eat Colin's food. Without the hotel element the business would be much less profitable. An alternative, which John's plan hinted at, would be to sell the West wing, removing bank charges but who would want to buy? After all, it had taken years to sell the property in the past.

The ultimate survival of the business would depend on the outcome of the complicated negotiations between Cornblend and Hammond and Cartland. No one knew how long they would take, but Roland Simister had suggested it might be several years, maybe as many as five. While the time seemed an asset, it could mean I would be living with uncertainty all throughout.

Chapter four

Kitty announced that she had arranged to work online and would stay on for the time being in Goosemere Hastily, we set about making one of the bedrooms habitable. I quite welcomed the physical effort. It did not take long, since my mother was happy to join in.

The room was soon transformed. Kitty chose a bed, which was delivered, and she was installed in her new bedroom within four days. There was only one electrical socket in the bedroom, so she commandeered one of the small tables in the corner of the bar as her workspace. She was therefore available to help whenever needed.

A call from John Stanwyck asked me to meet him in the bar at the end of the second week. He said he would pick up Roland Simister and they would arrive in time for Colin to cook them lunch before we could discuss one or two ideas. He would not be drawn as to what he meant by that. We could certainly do with some new thinking. Business was slack, except for the fish and chips. The arranged overdraft was already creeping up. The pressure had been eased, but Elsie's continued absence nagged at me.

John and Roland arrived as planned. I gave them both drinks while Colin prepared one of his special meals.

"What's this about?" I asked.

"After lunch, Tom," said John, "We'll explain everything then."

I had to be content with that, but I was already paranoid. Surely, these two were not also keeping secrets from me. I did not join them when their meal was served. Colin had produced an excellent meal which they clearly appreciated. I was, however, taken aback when they insisted on paying. John muttered something about 'tax-deductible' expenses. They congratulated Colin. Kitty, who was working at her computer, smiled, pleased for Colin.
John looked at his watch, then walked over to the door and turned the sign to 'Closed'. I wanted to protest, but I said nothing, just looking at him questioningly. He did not explain. He did not need to, for, at that moment, the main door was opened from the outside, despite the notice. It was a little late for lunch now, so it would be one of the 'sailors', dropping in for a pint, no doubt. Instead, it was Elsie. She was carrying a briefcase which she put down on the table Colin had just cleared. Then, she walked straight across to me and kissed me on the lips. I was gratified, relieved, even startled. Kitty looked delighted. My mother, who had just come downstairs from her room, looked mildly shocked. John and Roland averted their gaze, a little embarrassed.

"I've missed you," I said quietly before she pulled away and said, "Well, let's get this show on the road."

"What's going on?" I asked, not for the first time.

"We think," said Roland," we have a scheme which will save your bacon."

"We? Who's 'we'? Does everybody know about this except me?" I was annoyed. However well-meaning this intervention, I had been excluded. "Whose idea was this? Why wasn't I consulted at the beginning? I've had the impression that there was conspiracy going on behind my back. What gives you the right to interfere in my affairs without consulting me? You make me feel other people are taking over my life. I've had enough. Stop interfering, all of you!"

The annoyance had become out and out, unreasoning anger. I felt as a fighting bull must feel near the end of the fight, exhausted, bleeding from the multiple darts which had been hurled from all directions by picadors who were out of range. I could do nothing but bellow impotently.

They were all staring at me incredulously, all, that is, except Elsie. Her immediate reaction was to step back, as if I had struck her. Then her face assumed a stony expression.

"It was Elsie's idea," said John.

"Perhaps it would be better if we all sat down." It was Roland, older than the rest of us, except for my mother who was looking at me as though she had never known me.

We sat down. Kitty, Colin, my mother, and I sat on one side of the table, John, Roland and Elsie sat on the other side. Elsie sat between the two men. She was looking at me with the same, stony stare. We were like two, international chess grand masters, adversaries.

"Tom," Roland continued, once we were all seated, "I'm sorry you feel we've been going behind your back. When Elsie first came to us with this plan, none of us knew if it was workable. It is very complicated, as you will hear, if you listen. It would have been cruelty to have raised your hopes again only to see them dashed. Much of this scheme depends on factors outside our control. John and I both believe it could be made to work, but it has already taken a great deal of time and effort to establish that it is viable. Instead of being angry, you should be grateful that you have such friends. Elsie especially has spent many hours, many days, in fact, over the past two weeks, checking, canvassing support, seeking information."

I was already beginning to calm down. I tried to say I was sorry for my outburst, looking at Elsie, but I could not find the words.

"Since this is basically Elsie's plan," John said, "I think she should explain. Roland and I can attempt to clarify such details as we can."

Elsie had taken a sheaf of papers from her briefcase. She now put these in front of her, ready, no doubt, to give everybody a copy. She sat up straight, like a Victorian child in the classroom, her shoulders squared, and her gaze fixed unwaveringly on me.

"You have two, major problems," she said. "The most pressing is the lack of capital. That problem is reinforced by the unsustainable trading figures. You simply do not have a high enough income. There is not much chance of increasing the income for the immediate future. So, the second problem is how to continue to trade at a loss without allowing your debts to reach the point where you can no longer continue, or past the point where you will ever be able to regain control and get back into the black. Your original plan, as I – we – understand it, was to continue losing a little every year for approximately four years, by which time circumstances should be more favourable."

She was speaking like someone giving a presentation, as, I suppose, she was. It seemed bizarre. This was a small, intimate group of family and friends. She was addressing us as though we were a board.

"There was nothing radically wrong with the original plan. If you had not been faced by two problems one of your own makings: the first was that the unexpected collapse of the Cornblend Bank which removed the low-cost cushion which could have carried you through the first few years. The second, self-administered blow, was your decision to invest some of your own savings in the new kitchen. There is no way that this town can sustain a restaurant of the size needed. The food may be excellent, but there are simply not enough customers. I am not telling you anything you did not already know and which, I'm sure, John has already discussed with you."

I was squirming in my seat. It was as though I was being stripped naked again, only, this time, it was in front of more than just one person. The impersonal, emotionless tone of Elsie's presentation made the effect worse She spoke with authority, stating the situation as accepted fact, something beyond challenge. This was a person I did not know.

"Recently," she continued, "the government has made available a 'Coastal Town Recovery Fund,' which is administered by the Local Authority, in this case, the County Council. The LA can authorise locally a grant of up to £100,000 for projects which will enhance the community and make it more attractive to visitors and locals alike. The conditions are relatively straightforward. The most important of them is probably that any project must be partly funded by the proposers. That is to say, if the project were to cost, say, 100 K, the proposer would have to provide 50 K to attract the same amount of matched funding. I've brought copies of the details for everyone to read."

She was still staring straight at me impassively as she handed out some of the documents she had brought. I could not bring myself to look at them I was unable to look anywhere but her face. There was still no emotion in her voice or manner. I listened, but I failed to see how this funding could help me.

"This town," she continued, still looking exclusively in my direction, "has needed a Community Centre for a long time, a place where all the different social groups can meet. There has been a lot of demand for a youth club. My own Sailing Club is housed in a shack. Other groups hunt around for suitable accommodation. Among the papers in front of you I have listed some of these groups. They include obvious ones, like the WI, the Scouts, some clubs which are restricted in size because they have only small rooms, the Bridge Club, for instance. I discovered organisations I had not heard of, and I've lived here all my life. One group of retired men meet in a domestic garage as a Men's Shed. The school tries to accommodate same groups, such as Badminton, but they are compelled to charge for the use of rooms, including their hall, which is not only increasingly expensive, but the clubs also have to compete with the school itself. Some of the clubs and activities you can read about for yourself. I spent some time in Chelmsford, finding out if this new funding might be available for a Community Centre in Goosemere. I spent much more time contacting as many of these groups as I could, trying to gauge their reaction. The response was almost overwhelmingly in favour."

"It sounds almost too good to be true, Kitty remarked.

"There are two conditions attached to any award from this Fund," Elsie went on. She coughed. Colin fetched her a glass of water. She smiled at him briefly before she went on, her gaze, as before on me. "The first condition, I was given to understand, was no problem at all; any project must be one that will demonstrably enhance the town for the people who live here and for visitors. A Community Centre would certainly do all that. As well as the regular activities, it could offer somewhere for concerts, amateur dramatics, exhibitions. The second is the biggest challenge."

She paused to sip water. "What has any of this to do with me?" I asked for the first time.

"It is a question of matching funding".

"You're surely not going to propose I borrow the money for your scheme?"

She looked at me with a new expression. It was as though she was finding it hard to be patient with such a stupid suggestion.

"According to the valuation you had done recently, the West Wing of Harbour Lights is worth something over 100KK. If we could raise, say, just 50K, the matched funding would take us to 100K. You would probably have to sell below the valuation, but it would provide you with much needed capital, even after Tax, and the building could be repurposed."

I was stunned. I stared back. I was clearly expected to respond. I remembered that I was the last to be presented with this astonishing plan. I was being forced into a position. An unworthy thought crossed my mind.

"I realise this scheme could help with a cash injection," I said, "Nice to know, by the way, that everybody is so familiar with the state of my personal finances. But what's in it for you?" It was the question I had asked my father. No one would put in such effort from the goodness of their hearts. "And how would you raise the money?" I asked. "Have you anyone in mind?"

"That's the most difficult part of this plan," said John. "It's a community project. We wouldn't be able to find a wealthy philanthropist."

"The idea," said Roland, "would be to set up a Trust, a not-for-profit organisation. We could then begin a campaign to raise funds. It would need some good marketing. Your sister comes into it here. She has already sketched out a provisional website and would help co-ordinate a campaign in the social media."

Somewhere in my mind a penny dropped.

Elsie continued, "I have spent the past two weeks canvassing opinion," she said," Nothing specific, just seeing how people would react and if they would be prepared to put a little cash in. I was not specific about the venue for such a Centre, but I asked a lot of organisers of activities. The response was encouraging. A lot of people said they would willingly give money. It will depend on your willingness to sell. After that, the risk is ours. As for what's in it for me, I would be tempted to treat that question with the contempt it deserves, but there may be others who ask the same thing and, in any case. My reasons are what drive me and will, I hope, carry a lot of others with me. Apart from the years I spent at college, I have lived here all my life. I truly love this town and the people who live here. Many of them are my good friends. If I can help get a Community Centre, I shall be proud of it. The town is due to grow. I want to help improve it further."

Now all eyes were on me.

"I can't just say yes or no," I said. "I need time to think it over."

"But what have you got to lose?" asked Kitty. "You don't use the West Wing, can't afford to renovate it. It came to you as a gift. You will get much needed cash."

"What would be useful," said John, "would be a provisional agreement. A suggestion we have, if you feel positive about Elsie's plan, is that in a week's time we invite all interested parties to inspect the building. Those that respond positively would be asked for suggestions for adapting the space. We are aware of some changes that would be essential, such as the electricity supply. Some modifications to the structure would be desirable but would depend on costs. It would be good, for example, to knock the two, biggest spaces into one to make a decent-sized hall."

Elsie was still staring at me. This was too big for me. I got up abruptly and walked to the bar and poured myself a whisky.

"Does anyone else want a drink?" Colin asked.

I sat on a bar stool.

Kitty was showing everyone the proposed website, everyone, that is, apart from me and Elsie.

I did not know what to say.

"You are such an ungrateful sod." she said. "These people have given up time without counting the cost. They stand to gain nothing. John and Roland may well never be paid, and you haven't thanked any of them. Whatever your troubles, you should at least thank them It's different for me; if this Community Centre idea succeeds, my town, my friends will benefit."

"Elsie, I said, "I'm sorry. You're right, of course. I don't know what I think. I'm not sure I even know who I am any longer."

"No, nor do I," she said. "When you find out, get in touch. Goodbye, Tom."

She turned away, collected her briefcase, and walked out.

"Where has she gone?" Kitty asked. I shrugged helplessly.

"Tom," Roland said, "we need an answer, the sooner the better."

"I have no choice, do I? You'd better go ahead." At that I turned and headed up to my room. Kitty and my mother could see John and Roland out. I was past caring. Never had I behaved with such a total lack of courtesy.

From my room I was unable to hear anything. I lay on the bed, feeling that my world had ended, that the future would be meaningless, that I had lost Elsie. When Kitty knocked on the door and stepped inside, I told her rudely to go away. She didn't, however. Instead, she looked at me and asked, "What got into you?" We've sweated blood on this scheme. All right, so it will benefit Goosemere, if we can pull it off, but it will also save your skin. You stand to benefit, and more immediately. You haven't had to lift a finger. And you were so rude! You let John and Roland go without a word of thanks. You left Mum and me to say goodbye. As for poor Elsie."

"I've lost her, Sis!" I seldom called her Sis.

Instead of sympathising, she said, "If you have, it's your own fault. We all saw how she kissed you. No one kisses like that without meaning it. You will have to eat humble pie, I'm afraid. Elsie's too good to let her go without a fight. What on earth is this really all about?"

We seldom spoke this seriously or frankly. I knew she was right, but I seemed to have been faced many times of late by other people telling me truths I had to accept. I sat on the edge of the bed without speaking for a while. She said nothing more, just watched. At last, I stood up, took her by the shoulders, and kissed her on the forehead.

"Thank you, Kitty," I said. "I'm not in a fit state to talk to anyone tonight. Can I leave the three of you to look after things?"

"Why? What are you going to do?"

"I'm going for a walk to clear my head."

"You realise it's raining?"

"I'll wear a coat."

She gave me a worried look but left. I put on some old shoes and a tracksuit and went downstairs. Colin and Kitty were in the kitchen. My mother was nowhere to be seen. She had probably taken the dogs out. I took the familiar track up the hill as far as the farm gate. I stood there in the rain for a long time. I was soaked from the knees down and rain had trickled inside my collar. But I was no longer deeply miserable. I was doing my best to take an honest look at my behaviour, judging myself as a human being. The past year had been unusual and stressful. I thought of my time at Pilgrim's Rest, competent and, now I thought about it, complacent. Why else had my father's jibes gone home? I could not blame him for my move to Goosemere. It had been my choice, after all. And he had even warned me in a way to be careful, by admitting to his own carefree attitude towards the law. It was time to accept the past for what it was. More important still, I needed to deal with present problems. The scheme which Elsie had come up with was, according to my two professional advisors, was viable. It would depend on the ability of the team to raise money. I did not know how to do that. My reaction to Elsie's announcement had been like dousing it with icy water. It was ungracious in the extreme, ungrateful, as she had pointed out.

I turned back towards the town, squaring my shoulders, remembering how Elsie had done the same as she faced me across the table. The least I could do was to be positive, encourage this helpful, hard-working band. Their efforts, if successful, would help me to survive, maybe, but they would also create a new amenity for the town. If the pub failed, something worthwhile might yet come from these months of struggling.

Chapter five

My real education began in the next few weeks. The feelings of exclusion and isolation, though real, sprang from something inside me. Slowly, I came to identify this fundamental flaw. I had spent years learning the hotel business and becoming an efficient manager. Within the hierarchical structure of the business, I had learned many incidental skills, but the purpose was always clear; I wanted to be in control. Losing control, as now, was a disaster. Ever since the collapse of the Cornblend Bank, which had taken the rug from under me, I had been searching feverishly for a solution. This was my problem, as a good manager it was up to me to solve it. It was outside the scope of my thinking to hand over control. For the first time I was being manoeuvred into handing over. Also, for the first time, I was being forced to question my own motives.

Those who offered the rescue plan had been driven only in part by their wish to help me. The motivation which looked most likely to sustain them was the creation of a Centre for the local community. It was a type of lateral thinking in which I would benefit, almost incidentally. Elsie, and to a lesser degree my own sister, had already sacrificed hours of working time. John Stanwyck and Roland Simister had both worked in my interest, but they were prepared, it seemed, to offer advice and help to fulfil Elsie's plan. I was merely required to sell an unused building. The plan demanded little from me and promised to help my financial survival. My initial reaction to the scheme stemmed from the ignoble fear of losing control. My behaviour, self-centred, contrasted totally with that of the others. Elsie was right to be disgusted.

It was Kitty who made the next move. "Can we use the bar for a public launch on Saturday after -noon?" she asked.

"The bar? I suppose so. What have you in mind?"

She explained. It sounded like the meeting at which I had heard the scheme explained. John and Roland were ready to drive down for the afternoon. As soon as she had confirmed my agreement, Kitty would send out emails and work on the website. Elsie would spend the week like a political candidate, making personal calls on friends, businesses, and leaders of groups. Roland and John would attend the initial presentation here in the bar, where anyone could ask questions. If there was sufficient support, as seemed very likely, a steering committee could be elected. Roland would provide a sample constitution for a not-for-profit Trust group. The meeting would be advertised for 2 pm. Anyone sufficiently interested would be invited to look round the existing West Wing.

I told her to go ahead. I would ask Colin to provide tea and some orange squash. Kitty said that would be a good idea, but there was no money for catering. No, I said, this would be my contribution. She rang Elsie. I wished I could speak to her myself but instead I went to find Colin.

Now I was genuinely not involved. It was surprisingly difficult to stand on the touchline, watching the players running around excitedly, while my lone voice was carried away by the wind as I cheered them on.

There were no customers at all on Saturday morning. I put up the Closed sign just before 1 o'clock. Kitty and Colin began setting up a long table for the teas, and Elsie arrived with her briefcase. She commandeered a table to set out explanatory hand-outs. John and Roland arrived, and the party was complete. My mother, who had walked the dogs earlier, found a chair near Kitty. Conversation was a little strained, nervous. We were all remembering the last time we had met like this.

The first four people arrived ten minutes in advance, all four women. They were followed by a steady stream, mostly older people. Many knew Elsie and spoke to her. They called her Louise. No one wanted to sit down, it seemed. They stood in clusters and the room was soon full of noisy, amicable chat. By two o'clock the bar was full. I had anticipated serving tea for thirty, but there were many more. There was an old-fashioned bell over the bar. Elsie now rang it vigorously and the chatter ceased.

"Hello, everybody," she said. "Thank you all for coming. We didn't expect so many. You might be more comfortable sitting down, but I don't think we have enough chairs."

Soon all the chairs and benches were occupied. Some of the audience perched on the tables. About fifteen stood against the wall. Now they could all see and hear Elsie. She lifted a hand and the talking died. She introduced Roland, John, Kitty and me, then launched into her presentation again. Of course, she made no reference to the Harbour Lights other than to point out the changes we had made to the formerly derelict buildings. She was selling the idea of a Community Centre to a willing audience. She said the West Wing had recently been valued and that I was willing to let it go well under the market price. It would, she said, be my contribution to the Community Fund, if the project were agreed.

Roland took over, explaining the steps involved in establishing a Trust, suggesting the establishment of a steering committee.

John now explained how the project depended on matched funding. When he said we needed to raise £50,000, there was shock. Individual voices began to comment until Elsie held up both hands to demand attention.

"We know it sounds like a lot of money," she said, "but remember the Council will match it. There are a lot of people here. If each of you pledged say, ten pounds, we would already be on the way to the first thousand. If some of your clubs and associations pledged say, one hundred or more, even better. I am prepared to pledge the first five thousand pounds." She looked round the crowded room. "I've talked to a lot of you in the past few days," she said, "and several of the organisations you belong to have reserve funds. Think about it. Think of the advantages of having a place where all these groups can meet. We've prepared some hand-outs for you. Among them you'll find forms on which you can pledge donations of ten pounds or more."

"One important thing," Roland said. "The proposal is to establish a Community Trust. That will need a group of volunteers to act as unpaid trustees. Until such a Trust can be properly and legally constituted, we need to do two things: the first is to seek general agreement to go ahead, at least to explore it fully. Can we have a show of hands? How many of you are in favour?"

Virtually all the hands were raised.

"Good," said Roland. "Step two is to elect a Steering Committee. You will need a Chairperson, a Secretary and a Treasurer and I would suggest either two or four other members. In case you're wondering, I'm suggesting an odd number to avoid difficulties when voting in this committee. Again, I have prepared guidance notes for such a committee. The Treasurer should have a basic understanding of book-keeping, and the Secretary would be well advised to know how to use a computer. Are there any volunteers for Treasurer? That's usually the most difficult post to fill."

At this point I was surprised when a large, bearded man answered. "I would probably be interested. My name is Carter. I own the Thames barge and run a business, as most people know. I run residential training courses. I'm not sure how I might use a Community Centre myself, but I owe this town a lot. I'd join the Steering Committee if everyone agrees. I'll pledge a thousand pounds in any case."

Other volunteers came forward to fill the vacancies. Elsie was unanimously elected the Chairperson

"Just to remind you all," Roland summed up. "All this must be conditional upon securing the funding. If not, the organisation will be disbanded. If it succeeds, then the Trust will be formally constituted, and it will be up to the community. I wish you all luck."

"Before you go," said Elsie "Mr Hammond has kindly provided a cup of tea, you are also invited to explore the building we propose to convert. That is the West

Wing of the Harbour Lights, the range of buildings opposite this one across the cobbles."

At this there was a din of chairs being scraped on the flagstones, together with a babble of voices. The crowd swirled round the large, noisy room, some people heading directly for the tea, others collecting printed information. Roland and Elsie were surrounded by people seeking to speak to them. My mother made her way cautiously through the throng to look for the peace of her own room. I helped Colin and Kitty serve the teas. We were obliged to take some empty cups to the kitchen for a hasty washing up, not having prepared for such numbers. By counting the cups, I realised there were more than seventy people. At last, the room was clearing. I heard Roland speaking to Elsie. They were standing close to me.

"I think that was very successful," he said. "It will all depend on these pledges, of course. It is a lot of money."

"I hope it works," Elsie said. "This is something we've needed for years. But I don't know if we really can raise the money. Keep your fingers crossed for us and thank you so much for all your help."

"You do realise "Roland asked, "that John and I cannot be officially involved in the Trust? We are professionally involved with Tom, and that could constitute a conflict of interests."

"I hadn't thought of that."

"Well, until the Trust is constituted, we can continue to advise."

John and Roland took their leave. Elsie went out with them, answering more questions from the people who explored the proposed Centre.

I came back in from the kitchen and went behind the bar to wipe down the counter, where teacups had left wet rings. Five men came in. They were sharing a joke as they sat at the bar.

"Gentlemen?" I asked.

"Mr Hammond," said the tallest of the five," I'm Mike, these are Pat, Archie, Chris and Len," he pointed to each of them in succession, beginning with himself," carpenter, electrician, painter, plasterer and plumber." He laughed. "A painter, a carpenter, an electrician and a plumber walk into a bar," he said. I stared at him blankly. "You are supposed to ask, 'Is this some kind of joke?'" His companions laughed. "Now," he said, "if you pour us all a beer, we have an interesting proposition for you. Do we have to go on calling you Mr Hammond? What's your first name?"

"Tom."

"Right, Tom."

I pulled five pints. All five men watched, reminding me of the scene at the end of 'Ice Cold in Alex', when

John Mills watches the lager into the glasses. No one offered to pay.

"We are all retired," Mike said, wiping his lips with the back of his hand, "and for different reasons we all live on our own. For the past couple of years, we have been meeting at Archie's place most days to use his garage. He's the only one with a big enough garage to work in."

"Work in? I thought you said you were retired?"

"We are. We are working on a boat, trying to build one."

I must still have looked puzzled, because Chris explained, "It's what some people call a men's shed."

"Ah! I think Elsie might have said something about you."

"Nothing too rude, I hope," Mike said.

"It will be a long time before the Community Centre is up and running," I said. "If that's what you are going to ask. I'll have no say in how it's used, assuming it goes ahead."

"We realise that" said Mike. "By the way, you serve a good pint. Yes, we're not talking about the Community Centre idea."

"Oh?"

"We had a look, of course. There's a fair amount of work to be done, but there's a lot of potential. There are upstairs rooms as well as the ground floor."

The West Wing was the same length as the East Wing, where we now sat, but it was two stories high, not three. The two 'storerooms' used both stories, but four other sections all had two floors, so more rooms.

"While we were poking about," Mike went on, "we had a look through the windows of the other wing."

"The South Wing? That won't be part of the new Centre."

"No, we know that. We noticed the electrics had been done, though."

"They didn't do a very tidy job." Pat chipped in.

"The radiators are in place," said Len, the plumber." I imagine the solar panels are designed to help provide hot water."

I nodded, not sure where this was leading.

"Well now," said Mike, "it looks like the job was started but never finished. Am I right?"

"You could put it that way."

"Often happens on these big projects." The other four nodded agreement. "That's where we come in."

"You? I'm not ready to go ahead just yet," I said. "I simply can't afford it, to be honest."

"I told you, we're retired," said Mike." Our problem is that Archie's garage is small, its unheated. It can get very cold here." More vigorous nods. "What we had in mind was seeing if we might use a couple of the rooms in your South Wing. We couldn't afford to pay you rent, but we thought we could repay you in kind."

"What do you mean?"

"We have all the skills between us, as I said. We realise we couldn't use your place to build boats, but what about if we set about completing the work for you? We had a bit of a talk, and we are all ready to pitch in."

"But there's a lot of work needed."

"Yes, so what we thought was that in return for our labour you would agree to keep the rooms warm. No money to change hands, but one hot meal a day would be good, plus a pint, of course."

I was staring at him, astonished.

"You supply the materials. We have most of the tools we need. What do you think?"

All five of them were looking at me, awaiting an answer. I hesitated.

"Another pint while you're thinking would be good," said Mike. Automatically, I drew five more pints, not thinking about the cash. The five men waited patiently for me to think of an answer. My immediate reaction, once the sheer astonishment faded, was to do lightning calculations. If these men came five or even six days a week, I would have to find the cost of the electricity. That was modest, thanks to the solar panels. Five pints, and five meals a day would also be at cost. Decorating materials should not be excessive. It was always labour that demanded money, and these were offering to work without financial payment, so no PAYE.

"I don't have any guarantee that your work is up to standard," I said.

"Oh, now!" Mike reproached me. "We'll forgive you for that and not take it as an insult. What about giving us a week's trial? All you'll have to lose is a few snacks and the cost of a bit of paint."

I could not help liking them. "OK," I said, "One week, starting Monday."

Solemnly they shook hands with me, just as Kitty came in. I introduced them "My sister" I said.

"She's much prettier than you," said Mike.

I told Kitty what we had agreed.

"Well," said Mike, "See you Monday, eh, lads?" and they all signalled goodbye to Kitty and left.

"They're a great bunch," Kitty said.

"Maybe," I said, realising suddenly, "but they didn't pay for their drinks!"

I was not even annoyed, more like amused. Perhaps it was their determined cheerfulness, but they left me feeling more hopeful. It would be good to have them around.

When Kitty and I discussed it later, she pointed out that the investment in a few hundreds of pounds might soon be recovered. I could not see how. She said I might need to lower my sights again but, if the rooms in the South Wing could be made habitable, we could let them cheaply. I said that the renovations being planned for the Community Centre would make the Harbour Lights an unattractive place to stay for months. Even if the conversion were to be completed, some of the activities could well be noisy enough to disturb guests. Who wanted to come to Goosemere in any case? Kitty told me to be more optimistic and again she told me to lower my sights. "This will not be a luxury hotel," she said, not for a very long time to come, but, if you make the rooms really cheap, say half the charges you have been used to, I'm sure you'll get customers."

It was not what I had dreamed of, but beggars can't be choosers, and the very possibility of survival was an incentive.

My first instinct had been to label the men "The Magnificent Five', and the title stuck. I tried not to use it in their presence, as it suggested I saw them as cowboys. They were none of them young. I was to learn their ages ranged from 66 to 78. They turned up on the Monday morning in two, battered, old vehicles, obviously use for carrying all kinds of builders' materials. They brought their own toolboxes with them and put them down on the flagstone floor.

"Any old chairs or tables?" asked the one called Pat.

"There's the junk we cleared out of the bar when we arrived."

I led them to one of the storage spaces in the West wing. The men sorted through the heap of chairs, most of them broken and they found five which were serviceable. They would need a little cleaning. There was also a substantial table, which they seized upon with satisfied comments. They carried these trophies back to their ground floor workshop. I left them to it and went back to the bar.

At 11 o'clock Kitty, to my surprise, collected a tray, loaded with five mugs of tea, from the kitchen, together with half a dozen small packets of biscuits, and carried it over to the Magnificent Five. I followed. They had already cleaned up the furniture and the table now looked respectable. Their tools were neatly arranged. It was then that I realised they had chosen five stools to sit on, three-legged stools rather than four-legged chairs.

"Flagged floors," said Mike.

"What?"

"The floor is uneven," he pointed out." It's taken a long time to get the table steady." He pointed with his toe to one of the table legs, under which there was a neat wedge of wood, seemingly made for the purpose. "With three legs you will always be able to find a level spot, unless you plonk it down on a patch of soil, of course."

In the adjacent room they had made a start, sweeping the floor clean and filling the many small dents and imperfections in the walls.

"The plaster is not at all bad," said Len. He was a bit disappointed. His skills would be in less demand, and he would have to lend a hand with the other jobs.

They were grateful for the tea, although they had brought Thermos flasks.

"Drink up, lads," Mike said, as they replaced their mugs on the tray. "We can't let the boss see us slacking."

Kitty and I withdrew. As we crossed the cobbles, we heard them burst into song. They were singing an old, John Denver song, "Take me home, country road," and they were making a good sound, improvising harmonies.

In that week, we heard them many times. They were pleasant to listen to.

Promptly at one o'clock all five of them emerged into the courtyard. They beat dust out of their work clothes as they came into the bar. Kitty left her computer and directed them to a table under the window. I drew five pints and took them to the table, and Colin came out of the kitchen to speak to them.

"I take it none of you is a vegan?" he asked.

"No," said Archie, "we're all British."

Colin laughed. "I've done you a steak and ale pie," he said.

"Hope you've gone steady on the ale," said Len, "We've got to work again after this."

Colin gave up the conversation and enlisted Kitty's help to serve big platefuls of food. It was the first time they had been silent. They ate with something like veneration.

"Bloody hell!" said Pat, putting down his knife and fork. "That was great. Where did you learn to cook like that?"

There were appreciative murmurs from the others. For once the joking had been stopped.

"We weren't expecting anything like this," said Mike. It was almost as though they were embarrassed. They didn't stay long but thanked the three of us and went out into the courtyard, where Archie and Chris smoked a cigarette while the others breathed in clean air. Then they went back inside. I stood in the doorway of the empty bar as I heard a voice start to sing "Food, glorious food." I laughed. I was thinking how simple it was to give five, lonely. old men such a lot of pleasure. There may be nobody else to buy the food, but it had been served to a very appreciative bunch.

Roland Simister phoned the following morning. I was always ready for yet more bad news, whenever I heard his voice or John's. I was, therefore, not expecting him to begin, "Tom, good news!"

"What's that?"

"I've heard from your father's solicitors. They are no longer trying to get you to pay back the Cornblend loan. They accept liability on your father's account as the guarantor. He will now accept full liability. You are off the hook, my boy!"

I could not believe it at first. I said as much. Confirmation of the decision, Roland reassured me, would come in written form within forty-eight hours. I could not understand why they had changed their minds.

Although both Roland and John guessed the reason, I was not to learn the truth for over six years. By then my father had been found guilty of fraud and was serving a sentence in an open prison. I paid him a visit.

"Why the change of plan, you ask," he said, seemingly reconciled to a year or two 'at Her Majesty's expense', as he put it "It was becoming obvious by then the FCA was going to win the case. I was going down. That meant I would lose virtually everything I owned. I had already made over the house to your mother, so she would be OK. I also had some unreachable cash stashed away. (That's why I'll have to leave the UK as soon as I can at the end of my sentence.) It would serve no purpose to drag you under with me. In fact, leaving you to succeed down there in Essex would mean your mother, with any luck, would have an income of sorts from the two percent you had signed up for. I take it you are making a success of it now?"

I drove home after that, wondering how his mind worked, and hoping I had not inherited his cunning.

Before the Magnificent Five went home on that first day, Mike, who seemed to be their spokesman, came to me with a list of materials they needed. It included not only such stuff as cleaning materials, buckets, brushes, paint, but also, marked with a heavy question mark, timber.

"We thought," Mike explained, "we could build in a breakfast bar in the second room. These rooms won't be luxurious, more like a good quality hostel, so a communal space might be a good idea. We might be able to find some second-hand furniture when we've finished the decorating. What do you think?"

I looked at his estimated figures, written with the thick, carpenter's pencil he wore like a badge behind his ear. I had no way of knowing how accurate they were.

"Tell you what," he said. "If you put on some old clothes, you can come with me to help buy what we need. The cleaning stuff is essential, together with brushes, rollers, paint, and a few other bits. I'll sketch out the woodwork we were thinking about. Pat is also keen to spruce up the electrical fittings. Maybe we can take him along with us."

"OK," I said. "Remember, we want to keep the cost down."

"We'll stick to the essentials," he promised. "Don't forget; old clothes and a cheque book."

Perhaps it was Roland's news, but I felt far less stressed, despite being the owner of a business which was sinking steadily. I now proposed to indulge in a minor spending spree with two men I hardly knew, who were working for a hot meal and a pint of beer a day. I had yet to see the quality of any work. It could be that I might have to end this unusual arrangement at the end of the week.

I climbed into the front seat of Mike's old and dusty Volvo Estate the next morning. Pat was sitting in the back out of deference to me as boss, he explained. We drove to a builders' merchants, somewhere I had never been before, and we began with the simplest part of the list. Everything was cheaper than I had expected. Electrical light switches and ceiling fittings proved the most expensive items. The bill came to £645. We drove back to the Harbour Lights, several long pieces of timber wedged between the seats, making it difficult at times for Mike to find the right gear, but we got back unharmed. I left them to unload and went in to get myself a coffee and file the VAT receipts.

I looked in once or twice but left the five of them to get on with the work until Friday. It was decision time. I asked Kitty to come with me to decide if our agreement should continue. The room they had been using as their base and workshop was unchanged, though it was tidy. Buckets, paint, and various containers were arranged against the wall on a much-used, heavy-duty dust sheet to protect the floor, even though the floor itself was of stone flags.

"We've only finished one room," Mike said apologetically, leading us next door.

It had been transformed. The unsightly wiring was now buried in the walls, which were wonderfully smooth and painted a gentle shade of green. The window and door had been painted in a stronger shade of green, as had the skirtings. A section of one wall now held a work surface with a stainless-steel sink, plumbed in and a shelf above it. ("You can add cupboards later", Mike pointed out.) The workmanship was excellent, the effect, crisp and clean.

"I don't remember buying the sink," I said, thinking I would be facing another bill.

"Second-hand," Len said from outside the room. "I rescued it from a house a year or two back, when we were renovating the kitchen. It's been in the corner of my shed ever since."

It had been restored to look like new.

Kitty and I were impressed, but there were still more to see. These men obviously liked to work hard. They had stripped years of varnish from the bannisters leading up to the upper floors. This, too, looked like new.

"We had to replace one or two bits," said Mike. "It's work in progress, I'm afraid. We haven't finished sanding it down yet. And, as you can see, we haven't finished preparing the walls yet. We'll need another set of steps to reach the top of the stairwell."

I was staggered at how much they had achieved in five days.

"Well," Mike asked, looking at me with a mixture of pride and apprehension, "can we finish the job?"

"We love the grub," said Chris.

"The heating works well," said Archie. "It's great to be warm."

"You've done a great job," I acknowledged. "It would be good if you can keep up this standard. Do you think you'd be able to get the whole of one floor done? I need to be able to rent out the rooms as soon as possible."

"We can't guarantee a date," Mike said, "but we should manage one room a week. Then there's the stairwell and the corridor. Say ten to twelve weeks."

"You can't say no," Kitty said at my side. "Money will be tight, but this is your best bet."

"OK," I said. "Go ahead and thank you for what you've done so far. It must be on the understanding that I may have to stop if funds run too low."

"We hadn't realised there were money problems," said Mike.

"No reason you should," I said. "This place is not earning its keep as yet."

They were exchanging glances at this.

"We'd still like to go on," Mike said, "even if we have to do without the free meals."

"No! The agreement still will be the same. I can't let you work for nothing." I did not add that I knew just how much they enjoyed the simple but large meals. I guessed they did not relish the thought of returning to their solitary homes every night to a microwaved meal. It gave me pleasure to see them enjoying the food. I could see the relief at my decision. Kitty squeezed my arm to show her approval. The agreement had been reached.

We all adjourned to the bar, where I drew five pints and got myself a coffee.

"Cheers!" Archie said, raising his glass. They all drank thirstily. My phone rang and I excused myself to answer it, leaving the bar for a few minutes. When I returned, it was as the Magnificent Five were leaving. They shouted goodbye. The room seemed very quiet when they'd gone.

On the bar, under an empty glass, there were two ten-pound notes

Over the following weeks Elsie kept her distance except for the occasions when her Steering Committee met in the bar. Kitty continued to help with publicity. I tried to provide the Committee with some privacy, pushing some tables together so they could sit round them at the far end of the would-be restaurant area. There was little fear of customers eavesdropping. We seldom sold more than one or two dinners on the evenings they were available.

Gus Carter, their Treasurer elect, seemed to be a real asset. I was interested to know how the fun-raising was going but could hardly ask directly. Kitty, though helping, was not on the committee herself, but I asked her how it seemed to be going. She was reluctant to tell me anything at first, but eventually told me the launch had resulted in a really positive inflow of cash for the first four weeks before slowing down. She was publishing the results on the public media, which, as she knew, I never looked at. There was no point in her trying to keep them confidential. The original appeal reached the astonishing figure of pledged support of more than 35K, then it slowed to a trickle.

In another appeal on the social media and the website people were asked to help by staging jumble sales, coffee mornings, anything to raise funds. Elsie spoke to me before she chaired on of the meetings.

"We've had a suggestion from someone in the Amateur Dramatic Society," she said. "They've suggested an open mike evening. Could we stage it here?"

I don't know why, but when I had applied for my drinks licence, I had applied for a Live Music Licence. I supposed it had occurred to me I might hire a pianist or even a local band some - time in the future. It seemed ironic that the licence would be used to benefit everyone except myself."

"Thank you," she said. "You might even sell a few drinks."

The only hall in town was in the school, where there was no bar. Consequently, when the evening was announced, there was interest from the public. I could not charge for admission, but performers would be expected to pay five pounds to the Trust Fund, and there would be a collection. Members of the audience were asked to donate five pounds or more, if possible.

I tried to persuade the Magnificent Five to enter. They were not keen, but Kitty convinced them. They seemed to have a soft spot for her. As the day approached, we heard the quintet   rehearsing several familiar songs over and over. They were taking this seriously. Other entries came from individuals as well as from some of the Amateur Dramatic Society.   It promised to be a fun evening.

Three days before the Open Mike Concert, the Steering Committee held a meeting in the afternoon to sort through the proposed programme. That morning, as I finished sweeping the yard, Mike drove up in his Volvo with an aluminium ladder on the roof rack.

"For the stairwell," he explained.

"Where did you get that?"

"We borrowed it," he said. "They want it back for the weekend, so we'll have to get a move on."

Archie gave him a hand to carry the ladder inside. It was a three-part affair, the three parts telescopic, so it would fold to its present length of about ten feet. Fully extended, it would probably be the best part of thirty feet long. It looked brand new.

I thought only how enterprising they had been.

The Committee Meeting went on until nearly five o'clock. My mother returned from her walk with Shadrach, Meshach, and Abednego at ten minutes to five. They were not behaving well, pulling hard in different directions. One of the leads snapped. It was Meshack's. He was off in a flash. My mother shouted his name to no avail. He ran like the wind out of the courtyard and round the end of the East Wing. My mother, together with the other two dogs, rushed after him. I followed her, fearing what was to follow. My fears were realised as the dog rushed towards the river. My mother now screamed. She had to stop and hold the other two dogs as Meshak, unaware of danger, rushed towards the water. The tide was coming in, but not for another three hours. The wretched animal tried to run to the open water but, within a few steps his legs were sinking in the soft mud. He was about ten feet from the shore when he could no longer move, other than to make panicky, swimming motions. They served only to drive him further into the black mud. In a moment he could drown. I did not think. I ran after him, my own feet sinking until I was up to my thighs, but I reached Meshach, his eyes rolling in fear. I grabbed him, and with a movement which would have made an international rugby player green with envy, I wrenched him free and hurled him out of danger. He landed with a thud on the hard road. My mother, still shouting at the dog, seized his collar and dragged him towards the courtyard pulling Abednego and Shadrach after her. It was then that I realised the act of throwing the dog had driven my feet deeper into the mud. I was stuck fast. I was now nearly up to my waist, facing away from the road and I was still sinking slowly.

The screaming had drawn the attention of Gus and Elsie as they came out of their meeting. They took in the situation immediately.

"Tom! Don't move!" Gus shouted. I couldn't, as I shouted back, adding a few vulgar words. I heard someone running away. Elsie? No, Elsie was shouting, "Don't try to move your legs. Wait until we can help."

I did as she said. Maybe I was no longer sinking. It was hard to judge. What were they doing? I twisted round to try to see, causing Elsie to shout at me, but I realised some of the Magnificent Five had now appeared. It felt like an eternity before I heard more feet coming quickly towards the river. There was a metallic, clanking sound. I risked another look. Gus and Arche had brought the ladder from the South Wing and were now extending it. I was no more than ten feet from safety, so did not understand why they were extending it. At last came the scraping sound of the ladder being turned on the road surface. The top end was slowly pushed towards a spot just near my right elbow. I grabbed it with the nearest hand. I could only just reach the top rung with my left hand, but I was twisted, my chest at right angles to my waist. In this, awkward position, I could not exercise enough strength to pull myself round, but then I realised Elsie was lying face down on the ladder and crawling towards me. Three men were sitting on the far end to act as counterweights. Even so the ladder was flexing under the strain. She reached me and grabbed my left arm.

"We need to turn you round," she said, her voice sounding strange as she stretched to pull me. It was no good. Elsie was strong, I knew, but this was beyond her. She let go and retreated to the shore. There was a hurried consultation. Three of the Five ran back to the courtyard. They returned with what appeared to be sacks full of something quite solid.

They were doing something which involve the ladder again. I felt it move and it was soon at an angle, pointing downwards. The top was now near my ribs and below the surface. Elsie, now in danger of sliding down to join me, repeated her crawl. She reached me and told me to rest my right arm on the ladder and to grasp the rung furthest from me. She then grabbed my left wrist. She had turned her feet so that she had a grip on the ladder behind her, then she shouted, "Pull!"

At the other end of the long ladder, four men were now hanging on at waist level. The bags they had brought had been strategically placed on the hard surface, making an uneven seesaw. The ladder was bending under the weight of four men at the bottom and Elsie and me at the other. I felt that my shoulder was going to be dislocated. My ribs were under strain and very painful. But I felt my legs stretch as though I was on a medieval rack, and my feet began to ease very slowly until, with a sickening, sucking noise, I was free. Sobbing from the effort, I hauled myself far enough to cling to Elsie's body as the ladder slid slowly back to the bank. It had indeed buckled slightly. I stood up on shaky legs, clung to Elsie, tried to say thank you.

The two of us were black from head to toe. Gus left the others to clear up the road and fold the ladder as best they could, while he put a strong arm round our shoulders and took as back to the courtyard.

"We'll have to get hosed clean," he said. "Sorry it's so cold, but Kitty is organising a hot shower as soon as you're a little cleaner."

We were hosed down, using an outside tap with a hose attached. I gathered that the downstairs shower room, which we had installed for dog owners returning from a messy walk, had been monopolised by my mother and her precious dogs. Had Elsie and I been children, this might have been a game, but we were not children. I had feared I might even die. I was physically sore and aching. Elsie was equally exhausted, and her arms and back were hurting.

"This way," Kitty now led the pair of us up to my room. She directed Gus to my parents' room. Chris had collected two of the heavy-duty dust sheets from their workspace in the South Wing, and these had been spread on the stair carpet and in the bedrooms. Elsie and I shared my shower, the hot water streaming over us and starting to wash the filth from our clothes. It was no time for modesty. Awkwardly, in the confined space, we both dropped our clothes in the corner of the shower, passing the shower rose one to the other. We did not even notice through the steam, when Kitty came in with two large bath towels and two smaller ones.

"You'll have to lend me some clothes," Elsie said, as she stood, wrapped in a bath sheet, "And have you got a hair drier?"

"I used to run a decent hotel," I said, "Of course I have a hair drier."

I was almost too exhausted to get dressed. I sat on the end of the bed, watching Elsie dry her hair.

"Do you have to stare?" she asked.

I was hardly conscious I had been staring, but I was more than a little confused. Had she not told me on board the Moorhen that she didn't mind my gaze? I stood up and hunted in my wardrobe, finding a pair of jeans each, and two tee-shirts. I turned my back as I dressed, so as not to watch her. When I turned round, she was buckling a belt. She bent down and rolled up the bottoms of the trousers.

"Elsie," I said. "Thank you for saving my life."

"That's OK," she said. "It was a bit of a fright, but, thanks to Gus, it all ended well, more or less."

"I wonder what my mother will say when she finds there has been a strange man in her shower."

"Who cares? I can hardly believe she was so concerned for her dogs she left you in the river."

There were many things I was learning about my parents. I would not know the answer to Elsie's wondering for years to come, when my father had disappeared to live in South America. Shortly after that my mother was seriously ill. By the time I knew about it, she was dying. After the funeral, Kitty decided to research the family history. But that was a long way in the future.

Downstairs, Colin prepared hot chocolate for us, Gus chose a malt whisky instead. I thanked him.

"I learned something today," he said. "For years I've advocated using a ladder to rescue anyone from the mud. I need to refine that technique, it seems." He was referring to the courses he ran on the Cymbeline.

I also thanked the Magnificent Five and apologised for damage to their friend's ladder. They looked uncomfortable, as though trying to avoid my eye. I asked Mike directly to explain.

"We clubbed together to hire the thing," he said. "I don't think they're going to be too pleased, but you're still with us, that's what matters. Mind you, we didn't think things were so bad you'd want to throw yourself in the Gann. Good job you made a mess of it."

I told him of course I would compensate the hire company. He wanted to refuse, but I insisted.

We closed the bar early. Elsie, shuffling to Kitty's car in a pair of my flipflops far too big for her. Said goodbye with the lightest of touches, brushed my cheek with her lips, and left. I went to bed.

I was stiff and sore when I woke up the following morning. My arms and side were badly bruised, and I had hurt the muscles in my left side. I walked stiffly downstairs at half past eight.

"I should think so!" my mother exclaimed. "I nearly left without saying goodbye."

"Where are you going?" I thought she must have decided to go off on yet another shopping spree.

"Home," she said. "It's nearly six months. I don't want to risk anything like yesterday again. Thank goodness you got to Meshach in time."

Not a word about me, I noted this time, nor a proper thank you.

"I decided I want to get my boys home in our lovely garden. It will probably be badly overgrown by now. Stephan is supposed to be looking after it, but he's not the best of gardeners. Yes, I've been missing it more and more, especially since your father's been away. If we leave soon, we could be home by about one o'clock."

"You haven't given me much notice."

"Notice? What do you mean? Why do you need notice? I'm not asking you to drive me. Abednego, Meshach, come here!" The two dogs joined Shadrach, who was already standing next to her on the leash. She had prevailed on Colin to load her suitcases into her car.

"Well, I'll be off," she said. To Kitty she said, "Don't let him jump in the river again, Kitty. Take care of yourself. "She kissed my sister, allowed me to kiss her, and strode out to her car and her dogs.

Neither Kitty nor I discussed the sudden departure. I discussed with Colin the staffing of the fish and chip shop. It meant more hours for the casual staff. Kitty moved into the bigger room, but not until after the Open Mike evening. My escapade in the mud was reported on the social media platforms, complete with pictures, which were picked up in their turn by the local TV news. The item was less than a minute long, but the publicity was of disproportional benefit. The place was packed for the evening. The performances, as I had expected, varied from downright dreadful to surprisingly good. Several hopeful singing stars did their best, accompanied by badly played guitars, keyboards, pre-recorded backing tapes or unaccompanied, like the Magnificent Five. They were well received, and they enjoyed it. The Amateur Dramatic Society performed one or two mediocre sketches. The bar was busier than it had been since the opening night. I did not need to do so, but I donated a hundred pounds to the Fund. At last, the crowd left, still chatting as they crossed the cobbles.

"Do you mind if we count the takings in here?" asked Gus.

"Of course not."

I cleared one end of the bar and gave everyone a hot drink. There were three kinds of cash; the performers had each paid five pounds to take part, there was a collection in which the audience were encouraged to pay generously by putting money into a plastic bucket, and the Committee had made available more pledge vouchers. The performers, as was calculated in advance, paid £125. The cash in the bucket amounted to more than £400. Best of all, there were new pledges worth £500. The fund had edged forward a further grand.

Better things were to follow. The publicity generated by both the local TV report and the social media, when some of the performed acts were aired, revived the campaign. The Steering Committee continued to work hard and not having a suitable venue for such events, asked me to host whist drives, beetle drives, even another musical evening at which the more popular performers were invited to return The funds raised was deposited in a special 'Community Account'. Which would be used to benefit about ten named local charities if the appeal failed. Most of the Appeal funds remained only pledges, but the two sums were steadily growing. The most encouraging part of all this was the success of the online publicity.

I was about to close the bar one lunchtime when a stranger walked in and ordered a beer. He was a smartly dressed man of about fifty. He sat at the bar, seemingly ready to make conversation.

"Are you the owner?" he asked.

"Yes, Tom Hammond. Your accent, South African?"

He nodded. Yes," he said, "though I was born here, lived in Goosemere until I was ten."

"Oh?"

"We emigrated to South Africa," he said. "I happened to look for Goosemere on my browser a while ago and saw the website about the Community Centre. Am I right in thinking it's going to be here at the old pub?"

I explained, but, when he began praising the website, I gestured towards Kitty and told him she was my sister. He went over to her then and asked a few questions before coming back to his seat. "Can I have a look at the part you're planning to convert?" he asked. "Who has the keys?"

I explained the West Wing was still mine, that we were waiting until the Fund was big enough, that I would love to be able to donate the building but could not afford to. "I've agreed a very low price," I said.

I collected the keys and asked Kitty if she'd like to join us.

It was a far from cursory visit. Martin Hendrick, as he introduced himself, was intent on something more like an inspection. He asked many questions, some of which neither of us felt competent to answer. He asked how we proposed to create a decent-sized hall from the two, separate spaces. He asked who the architects would be, who was drawing up the necessary plans and what we planned to do about parking. I locked the final door and led the way back to the bar.

"Thank you both," he said, making no move to sit down again. "From what I've seen, I'm ready to make up the difference between what you've raised and the target."

We both stared at him without speaking. He laughed. "You remind me of two goldfish in a bowl," he said. "Which of you can take the money?"

"Are you sure you realise how much we're talking about?" asked Kitty.

"I think so. It amounts to about five thousand British pounds, I think."

"Neither of us is the person to take your money," I said. "We're not part of the Steering Committee."

"Oh, who should I be speaking to?"

Elsie might not be in her shop. "The Treasurer is a man called Gus Carter," I said. "He lives on board the Cymbeline, the big Thames barge. You probably saw it when you came in."

"I'll take a little walk up there then," he said.

"The road's very muddy," I warned him, looking down at his town shoes.

"A bit of mud never hurt anybody," he said.

I bit my tongue at that, and Kitty said she would walk with him to introduce him to Gus.

"What do you think about that?" she asked me, sparkling with excitement when she returned. Mr Hendrick did not return. I cleaned some tables and the bar. If this man did as he said he intended, the Fund would reach the target and the formal application could be made. Doubtless the Committee would have to wait a while for confirmation. A lot would need to be done, even before the sale could be legally agreed. I hoped I could survive that long, as I might easily reach the limit of the agreed overdraft by then My only hope was for trade to improve. The most infuriating feature now was that the Magnificent Five had done all they could in the South Wing. To complete that part and render it profitable, it needed floor covering as well as basic furniture. There were ten bedrooms ready. Beds, mattresses and the cheapest of wardrobes – Mike had even suggested they could build them - would come to at least £2,500. Floor coverings would cost about half as much again. I simply couldn't afford it. So near, yet so far, I told myself despairingly.

Kitty remained excited that the Centre Appeal was going so well. She and Elsie were good friends now. Elsie had warmed towards me but treated me more as a friend. I often thought just how shocked she had been at my angry outburst. We hadn't talked about it, but her reaction, when I thought about it, had been out of proportion. At least we were back on amicable terms, though she was even busier than before. She and her Committee were quite able to complete the Application, since there were people on the Committee with previous experience, both in contractual and in financial matters. When all was in place, nevertheless, they sought final help from Roland. He came to one of their meetings in the bar. It felt odd to watch him take his place at the other end of the room.

When the meeting broke up, he spoke to me. It would, he said, probably take a further three months at least before any money could be paid into my account, maybe longer.

As he was telling me the bad news, the Magnificent Five, who were finishing off the work in the South Wing, could be heard singing. He asked who the singers were. I told him. Until that moment he had known nothing of them or our agreement. He looked worried all at once.

"Can I have a look at what they've done?" he asked.

"Of course," I said, and walked with him to the South Wing. I imagined his anxious look was down to doubts about the wisdom of employing casual workers to restore a building. I introduced him to the Five, who watched as I took him from room to room. They were clearly and justifiably proud of what they had achieved. Roland said nothing, but he appeared to find the work far better than he had anticipated.

"Thank you," he said to the Five as we left to go back to the bar, " Impressive. Well done!"

I sensed there was more to be said, however.

"Did you say these men all volunteered, that you don't pay them?

I explained our bargain, a warm workshop, one meal and a pint of beer a day.

"That constitutes a form of contract," he said. "You are employing them. Albeit payment is in kind, and well below a minimum wage. Do I take it they call themselves self-employed?"

"No, they call themselves retired," I said, wondering what was coming next.

"What about insurance?"

"What are you asking?"

"You should have insurance cover for them unless they each have their own. They're not exactly in the prime of life. Since you are, in the eyes of the law, employing them, you are liable for injury, loss or even death caused while in your employment."

This came as the worst possible news.

"If you want to avoid trouble, you must end this agreement until you can find someone willing to insure you. I don't hold out much hope, in view of their ages."

Again, my mood had bent like that aluminium ladder, and I was slowly sinking into total despair. No matter how hard I tried and however many helpers tried to assist, I was heading for failure. The Harbour Lights was dragging me down, clutching at my ankles. It made things worse that the Community Centre now stood a high chance of success. It could well be that the Centre would be opening with joy and celebrations on one side of the courtyard, while the other two wings were left in darkness. Kitty was chattering excitedly on the phone to Elsie. I took myself out for a walk. I did not want to spoil the moment for others.

I passed the Cymbeline and walked on. It was beginning to grow dark. My phone rang in my pocket and I was tempted to ignore it. If it was Elsie, the last thing I wanted was to depress her. But it was Tony.

"I hear congratulations are in order," he said.

I did not understand. "Kitty tells me you have the money for the new Community Centre," he said. "So that means they will soon be able to buy the West Wing, doesn't it?"

"That is the plan, yes."

"You sound less than pleased, Tom. Isn't this what you've been waiting for?"

"It's not quite so simple," I said.

"Haggling over the price?"

"No, nothing like that."

I had reached the farm gate. I stopped in order to continue the conversation. I noticed there was movement at the other side of the big field, what looked strangely like a large caravan.

"Megan is in the bath," Tony said. I wondered why he felt he had to tell me that. "I can talk for a while. Explain yourself."

I explained how near I had been to finishing the South Wing and to earning some useful money. I told him the sale would not go through for perhaps three months, and that by then I would run out of money.

"Didn't you tell me you had negotiated an overdraft?"

"Yes, but it won't be enough for the furniture and flooring."

"How short are you?"

"About five K."

"Sorry, Tom, I'll have to ring off for a moment. Can I call you back?"

"OK. I'm not going far." I pressed the Off button.

I stared across the field, wondering if the farmer had permission to put caravans there. It was an isolated place, in any case.

I was halfway down the hill when Tony rand back. "Tom," he began, "Megan and I have talked. Are you positive about selling the West Wing?"

"As sure as I can be. Everyone seems to think it's a foregone conclusion. They've been assured by the Council that the Grant will go through on the nod. Why do you ask?"

"We were going to buy a new car," Tony said, "but we can wait six months. We've got about ten thousand saved."

"You can't do that!"

"We can easily lend you five thousand for six months, even longer if need be."

"I couldn't take your money!"

"I must say this is a difficult discussion to hold on the phone, and it sounds as though you are outdoors."

"I am."

"Tom, I am going to insist. Megan is in full agreement. It's what families do, help one another. The money would only sit in our account and the interest rates are so low, you could at least make it work for its keep."

I argued a little more until he said, "Tom, say yes or I swear I'll draw the money in cash and drive down and stuff it in one of your apertures."

"Tony, I can never thank you enough for this. I'll say yes, but I'll pay one percent over the bank rate."

"Now you're sounding just like Dad," he said.

"God! I hope not! It was Dad who landed me in this mess."

"You know, Tom, Kitty and I have often wondered why both Mum and Dad seem to treat you differently from us. Well, Mum does especially, I'm not so sure of Dad. He's never been very affectionate to us either. After all, you'd think he'd know what he was doing when he gave you the Harbour Lights, but Kitty says Mum left you sinking in that stinking mud after you'd rescued Meshach."

"I've sometimes wondered if I was adopted, you know."

"Adopted? Surely not."

"It just feels like that at times."

"Well, look, the cheque is in the post, as they say."

"I don't know how to thank you, you and Megan."

"Don't try. Just take care and do steer clear of that mud in future. Maybe we can come and see what you're doing with the place at half term."

I almost skipped the rest of the way. Indeed, I felt like a coiled spring which had been compressed and suddenly released. An image of Zebedee in the Magic Roundabout came to mind, and I jumped, shouting "Boing, boing, boing!" until the pain in my ribs returned and I coughed and laughed like a madman. As I straightened up I realised Gus Carter was standing on the deck of the Cymbeline, smoking a pipe. He was watching my antics with amazement.

Early the next morning I was waiting for Mike and the others and went inside with them. They wondered why. I asked them all to sit because I had something to say. The elation I had felt was tempered by new worries which Mike sensed.

"You look like you've got more bad news," he said. "Are you planning to kick us out?"

I told them what Roland had said about insurance.

"But you're not employing us," Chris said.

I explained further.

"Well," said Archie, scratching his head. "I don't think it would be fair to expect us to carry on without some sort of Kid pro co."

"Quid pro quo." Mike corrected him absent-mindedly.

"We don't need insurance," said Pat. "We're not going to have a serious accident with a paintbrush."

"Electrics is different."

"Granted, but we all know what we're doing."

"I suppose this was bound to come to an end sooner or later," said Mike. He spoke directly to me. "If you can't afford to furnish this place, you wouldn't be able to use us anyway. Tom, we're grateful for your help."

"Hang on!" I said "I can finish the furnishing now -an unexpected windfall. If I can find guests to occupy this wing, I might be close to breaking even. I was hoping, if it worked out, that I might ask you to take on the East Wing. The top floor hasn't been looked at. We've only refurbished half the first floor."

They all looked much brighter.

"That will keep us going for a while," Chris said.

"But I still can't afford to pay you," I said quickly. "Also, there's still the insurance problem. I take it none of you has a personal insurance?"

"We don't need insurance."

"I cannot risk it," I said. "You're welcome to use this room, but no work. I'll investigate."

"At least we can keep warm," said Archie.

"Thanks for being straight with us," Mike said.

"We'll be able to use the little kitchen, I take it?" Len asked. "We can always make toast and heat up some soup."

"We can't build a boat here, though," Archie pointed out.

"Colin has already got the supplies for today," I said. "Stay for lunch. I'm off to find out what I can about industrial insurance."

I left them, five men, hunched round a scrubbed, deal table, perched on three-legged stools. All at once they seemed older, more vulnerable.

I told Kitty and Colin I had to take the van to Chelmsford. I explained that Roland had told me to sort out insurance. I left it deliberately vague. I had little hope I'd be able to arrange cover. Even if it proved possible, it would surely cost the earth. Taking the ages into account, I suppose my thinking was influenced more by quotations for car insurance. I suspected I would be asked for several thousands of pounds.

I found a small office in a Victorian building. There were three people at computers in the room as I entered. A young woman asked if she could help. I told her I wanted information about industrial employees. She frowned an picked up a phone, spoke to someone in another office. She scarcely had time to replace the receiver before a door opened and a thin, bespectacled man appeared. He was in his fifties, I guessed, and he asked me to go into his inner sanctum.

I sat across the desk from him. He also had a computer which was at right angles to me. It was turned off. I told him my name and began to explain what I was about. He interrupted me, sounding curiously excited.

"Mr Hammond? Mr. Thomas Hamond?" he repeated.

"Yes," I admitted, puzzled. I had never seen this man before.

"You've come from Goosemere?" I said yes.

"I thought I recognised you! He said, " You're the man who risked his life to save that dog!" Again, I couldn't deny it, though I had not seen the incident in quite that light.

The man was a fervent dog lover, he told me in an hour's conversation. Mr Ken Crampon's name was written in gold leaf on a wooden stand on his desk as well as a plastic badge. I wondered if he needed to remind himself of his name or was eager to promote himself. He was more lecturer than conversationalist. He lavished praise on me for my heroism, spoke of the TV report, and of the social media pictures and discussions. He then talked at more length of the dangers presented by rivers and by the Gann in particular. He described some of the claims he had read which had been occasioned by similar incidents.

At length he said, "But let me see, now, how can we help you?"

I explained in a few sentences.

"Well, now," he said, and I steeled myself for a further lecture. "I think we should be able to fix you up. We needn't worry too much about how old your employees are, if they are properly qualified."

I assured him that they were.

"I can do you a one-year cover, then," he said. "Let's say fifty pounds plus tax."

I looked shocked.

"I'm afraid I couldn't possibly make it lower than that," he said, misunderstanding.

"No, that will be fine," I said.

"I'll draw up the proposal for you and send it. If you agree and can get it back to me with the premium by the weekend, I'll make the start date next Monday."

I thanked him and stood up, fearing he might go on talking. He came to the door with me and through the outer office, telling me it was a privilege to meet me. Outside, I returned to the car park and drove home, smiling at the successful outcome, but partly at the memory of the odd man who had talked so long.

I lost no time in giving the Five the good news. They could have a week off, I said, "A week on paid leave." I was feeling generous, and they would have one good meal a day instead of soup and toast.

Chapter six

Two weeks later we were ready to open the South Wing. Kitty was quite right we soon had all the rooms filled. This was not simply down to the very low charge, as I told her, not wanting her to boast about it. She it was who advertised on our website (which she had also designed.) These were all single rooms and were advertised as simple, clean, and basic. They were cheaper than all the bed and breakfast accommodation Kitty could find locally. For once I was lucky with my timing. When I had been standing at the farm gate, talking on my phone to Tony, I had noticed a large caravan on the far side of the field. I forgot about it afterwards, but I learned this was the first sign that the Agronomy Research Station was starting. They would soon be building some administrative blocks, greenhouses and laboratories. While this work was about to begin, a small band of workers were already preparing experimental plots and sowing seeds. These people, men and women, needed accommodation.

I learned a little about agronomy from conversations in the bar, where these workers also helped my profit by having a drink or two. They were highly qualified scientists, not as I at first assumed, horticultural labourers. They worked long hours, so they were no trouble for me. They set off for work in a minibus before seven o'clock. Colin served an early breakfast, a full English, at 6.15. The rooms were free for two part-time ladies to deal with when they arrived at ten. I was unaccustomed to providing single room accommodation, but found a big advantage was smaller sheets and duvets. Washing and drying was easier.

I charged just £65 per night. Full occupancy generated £650 per night, or £4,550 per week. Despite the added labour costs, for the first time my accounts were looking healthy, healthy enough for me to pay Colin a small salary which, I promised I would increase substantially in time. I was in my element, managing three businesses at the same time, the fish and chip shop, the South Wing, and the bar. I was obliged to take on more staff there too, but I was beginning to climb back into profitability. I was very busy.

Kitty had given up trying to combine working for her agency as well as from her improvised office in the corner of the bar. She had added to her own workload by dealing with the Harbour Lights website, also the Appeal Fund. I relieved her of helping with the bar. Kitty had enjoyed it, but she had been working all day and in the evenings. When it came to employing bar staff, I was careful, knowing this was an area where dishonest employees could have a hand in the till. I took on two youngsters, both female students, Chloe and Eva. They were popular and honest, as I soon found, as I cashed up during the first weeks. I was not out of the woods yet, but the trees were a little better spaced.

Freed from bar duties, Kitty moved into the empty room next to her bedroom to use it as an office. Pat installed not just an extra power point, but a separate circuit and fuse box, with multiple sockets. He also set up a separate modem and wi-fi. Kitty changed her laptop for a bigger, desktop machine. She and Elsie were now firm friends. Elsie, also busier than ever, made frequent visits, but her business being with Kitty, she seldom said more to me than "Hello" as she passed through. I was not always at the bar, anyway.

The Five got on with their work, but I did not want the same kind of renovation there. The rooms in the East Wing would, if all went well, become good quality, double rooms, furnished and decorated to a high standard. The doubts I had expressed in the past concerning the probable lack of demand, had been completely reversed. I did not allow myself to think I might be too optimistic.

When I discovered the Agronomy Station was on its way, I did what I should have done weeks earlier; I checked out the Development Plan. It had been available for public inspection for some time by then and it was now too late to register any objections. What I found took me completely by surprise. Heavy, earth-moving equipment had already moved into the bottom, narrow end of a field adjacent to the main road where it forked. I realised, seeing a row of surveyors' poles, that a road must be planned to take traffic off the T-junction and up the hill to the Agronomy Station. It looked like an expensive plan. When I examined the full Development Plan, however, it made more sense, although it came as even more of a surprise. I had imagined that the proposed, residential estate would be on the far side of the town. It was planned instead to be built on land on either side of the new road, which ran south-west from the bottom of the hill to the Agronomy Station. A new school and a small row of retail outlets would be included. It meant that the centre of the new look Goosemere would be close to the Harbour Lights and the Community Centre. I stared at the plans in the library for nearly an hour. My father had been right all along. It was a matter of time before all the anxiety and struggling would bear fruit. I would own a property in a prime position. I could hardly believe it. I had been so preoccupied, the first time I glanced at the plans, that I had only looked at the sheet showing the housing development, and I had not looked at the overall scheme.

"What are you going to do for your birthday?" Kitty asked at breakfast.

"I haven't thought about it," I said.

"Well, things are definitely looking up, and you've been working your socks off all year. I think you should celebrate, throw a party."

"I think my party days are over."

"Don't be such an old sourpuss. At least let some of us have a bit of fun."

"Some of us? How many were you thinking of?"

When I thought about it, I could think of very few people I could or wanted to invite. I had arrived in Goosemere, knowing I had made few real friends, only colleagues. Not much had changed. Of course, Kitty would be a guest, and I would like Elsie to come but unless I asked John and Roland, who were really business associates rather than friends that left only Colin.

"What about the famous five?" Kitty suggested.

"I'm not sure they would want to come, even if I asked them. Although they would probably enjoy another free meal, but they wouldn't be able to get back home in the evening. Judging by the way in which they quaff my beer. I don't think they would be able to drive. They would probably refuse, even if I invited them. It hardly seems worth the effort to hold a dinner party for just four of us."

"Of course, it's worthwhile!"

Colin was quite happy, given enough notice, he said, he would be able to prepare the food in advance and leave it to his assistant to serve, provided there were no other customers. As it happened, my birthday fell on a night when the restaurant service was not available to the public. For once Colin would eat his own food with us. It was only a small party, nevertheless.

When I came down to the bar that evening, I found that Colin and Kitty between them had done a good job in decorating the table at the far end of the bar. Wine glasses sparkled on the bright, white cloth, reflecting the flames of four candles. The bar itself was open and about five or six agronomists came in for drinks during the evening, served by Chloe. We had the place to ourselves otherwise. As was normal, I had received only half a dozen birthday cards, including those from my three guests and from Tony and Megan. There was one from Mike on behalf of the Five. We took our places   Kitty had bought me a new wallet. Colin presented me with a small packet. It contained a splendid, silver pen I thanked both. Elsie reached under the table and pulled out a cardboard box, covered in gift wrap. It was about 12 inches square and 15 inches high. I thanked her and unwrapped it. Inside the cardboard box there was a lot of packing which ended up on the floor as I slowly revealed the contents of the box which was one of Elsie's figurines. I lifted it carefully and set it down on the table where everybody could see it. It was a model of a naked man, his back towards me. He was standing on one leg, trying to balance while he pulled on a pair of pants. His left hand was braced against a doorway which, when I looked carefully, I recognised. It was the door of the cabin on the Moorhen. The figure was trying to balance in the small cockpit. Although he had his back to us, he was looking uncomfortably behind him, and it was very clearly my face. Everyone laughed at the workmanship was exquisite I felt myself blushing. Elsie stooped and kissed me on the cheek, saying, "Happy birthday!"

The laughter subsided. "Colin," I said, "I think it is time I said publicly how much I appreciate everything you have done since you came here. It has not been a very easy time for any of us, but you stuck with us heroically, even when I suggested you might like to leave and look for another post. I haven't been able to show you how much I appreciate the fact. I want to make a proposal."

Colin looked embarrassed and tried to laugh it off. "I won't marry you," he said. "That's going too far."

"Colin," I said "at present the Harbour Lights is registered as a company with myself as the sole director. What I'm proposing is that you join me as another director. We can work out the terms later, if you agree in principle. It will still be a year or two before you really gain financially. I hope you will agree, however, because I feel you have more than deserved it. Think about it. If you are interested in the idea, we'll get Roland Simister to explain exactly what is involved and to draw up a proper agreement."

Colin was staring at me, open mouthed. "Are you serious?" he asked.

"Of course, I am. It has been pretty evident of late that I need other people or at least one other person to help make the right decisions."

Kitty was looking at me with an expression I had never seen on her face before. Her eyes were shining, almost tearful.

Elsie, too, was looking at me. "Well done, Tom," she said quietly.

The soup arrived, and we began to eat. There may have been just four of us, but the mood was a happy one. Perhaps the wine helped a little. The bar had emptied. Colin thanked me for the evening, said he had to be up early, he would think about the proposition, but he was decided already. He was honoured to be offered the opportunity. We would discuss it properly in the morning, I said. Colin went out to the kitchen, checking that everything had been left in order. It had. By now it was quite dark. He wished us goodnight and said he was off to bed. Elsie seemed to want to linger awhile. Kitty gave both of us a quick glance and said she would be off, too. Elsie and I were left in the bar.

"Can I stay over?" she asked. I was startled.

"I'm not sure we have a room ready," I said. "I haven't had more than a couple of glasses of wine, I can drive you home, if you like."

"Don't be so obtuse," she said, "I need to talk to you."

"We've been talking all evening," I said, deliberately misunderstanding her.

"We'd be more comfortable in your bedroom," she said. Without more ado, she turned and began to mount the stairs. Hurriedly, I turned off the lights, checked that the door was locked, and followed her.

She was sitting, fully clothed, on the bed, propped against the headboard.

"Don't put the light on," she said. I looked at her, wondering what she had in mind. She patted the bed inviting me to sit next to her, as one invites a dog to join you on a sofa. I kicked off my shoes and sat beside her in the light from the full moon. A faint breeze moved the curtains from time to time chasing shadows on the bed. The window was partly open, and the river, which was full, could be heard as the waters swept over the mud. We sat for a few minutes, not touching.

"You have changed," she said. "For the better, I should say. When you first arrived in Goosemere, your attention was entirely taken up with turning this place into a prosperous hotel. I thought then that your ambition was stronger than your chances of success I watched as the struggle of your life began to swamp you. I remember the day when you came fishing with me."

"I never forgot it."

"No. Nor did I. But then things went badly wrong. I'm thinking of that dreadful day when John Stanwyck ,Roland Simister and I tried at last to offer a plan which might save you."

"And I lost my temper and my senses I remember only too well"

"You thought we had been conspiring together."

"Yes"

"I suppose we were in a sense. We didn't tell you what we had been discussing until then. We all believed you would grab the opportunity we were offering and be grateful. It was a realistic plan, and I had been sweating blood for the previous two weeks to make sure it would work."

"Elsie, this is all in the past. I need you to forgive me and to move on. Do we have to go over it again? It has been a good evening up to now."

"I have to explain," she said. "I owe you that much. I'm sure you must have noticed how my behaviour changed."

"I realised I had offended you. I was completely ungrateful. I swore at all of you and stamped out, if I remember."

She nodded in the semidarkness. "Offended is not really the right word," she said. "Of course, anyone would be hurt to have a decent rescue plan thrown back in their face, but it was more than that. You see, nearly six years ago now I was deeply in love with a chap called Simon."

"Oh!"

"Yes, it was the real thing. I would have done anything for him. He was certainly in love with me, it seemed. I was beginning to make a real success of my pottery at this time. I had discovered at last that the best way forward was to attend craft fairs all over the region, as I still do. It meant staying away overnight for most of the fairs in question. One day I noticed a man I didn't know, poking around one of the stalls I realised I'd seen him at the previous show. Nothing very strange in that, I suppose. But then he turned up at the third show in succession. He seemed a bit odd. He was there for the entire afternoon, looking around from stall to stall, but not buying anything. I began to feel he was following me. It was creepy. I asked a couple of the other exhibitors if they had noticed him. They had. I tried to find out who he was, and I took a picture. I suppose it's strictly speaking illegal, but I posted it on Facebook and asked if any of my friends knew the man. One of them did. He was a private investigator! I was really scared now. Who would want to have me followed, and for what? I won't explain how I found out, but it was Simon who had contracted this scary little rat to watch me. I went mad. The man I loved and who said he loved me had proved so jealous, so possessive that he thought I was being unfaithful. Or was it that he wanted to own me, to have total control? When I faced him with it, we had one almighty fight and I have never seen him since."

"That's dreadful," I said weakly.

Elsie had not moved. She was speaking into the darkened room as though making a confession. She had not finished. "By the time I came up with the idea of creating the Community Centre to help you financially as well as to do something useful for the town, I thought I might be falling for you. Your reaction came as a direct reminder of my experience with Simon. I had made – or I was close to making – another, terrible mistake. I had misjudged you completely. But you told me once that you wanted the complete control of ownership rather than managing a hotel. I needed to pull back. I'm sorry."

"I behaved appallingly," I said. "The bottom seemed to be dropping out of my world. I was going to lose everything. I think I was close to a mental breakdown. I have often thought I was literally out of my mind, unwell. I am so sorry."

"I can see that now," she said. "It would probably have been better to tell you what we were up to instead of keeping it secret. The trouble was that none of us knew if it was even remotely possible. That's why I spent weeks investigating. We were all concerned for you."

"If you hadn't thought of this scheme," I said, "I would certainly not have survived. As it was, I had to readjust even with the prospect of a long- term solution, things looked black for a while. I realised that my ambition to own and run a high-class hotel was never going to work here in Goosemere. It couldn't work – still can't – not until the town has developed as my father, God rot his soul, forecast it would. The way things were, I could never survive that long. If I did survive, it would not be in the capacity I had hoped for I might manage a second-rate establishment. Running a fish and chip shop was the last thing on my mind. The things which have worked have almost all been because other people suggested them - that, and the completely undeserved loyalty of you, Kitty, Colin, John and Roland"

"And that is how you've changed," said Elsie. "You have accepted that you cannot solve your own problems without help. And tonight, when you offered Colin the opportunity to be part of your company, that was a huge change. If he accepts, as I'm sure he will, you will have to listen to him and to the rest of your friends. People already know you are making over the West Wing at well below the market value. They appreciate the fact. You have already found their respect."

I did not say anything more.

"It's getting chilly in here," Elsie said, "can we at least get under the duvet?"

We moved and this time we lay down and pulled the duvet over us, not bothering to undress. I turned to her and took her in my arms. I kissed her and realised her cheeks were wet with tears. I wiped them away.

"What's this about?" I asked, as I wiped her face.

"I've ruined things," she said. "I shouldn't have reacted as I did when I

 did. I am just hoping we can find some way to remain friends."

"I think you must forgive me. I have been so wrapped up in my ambitions and fears, I have treated you and others so badly."

So, wrapped in one another's arms, we fell asleep. It was very late. We awoke at 5 o'clock, still tired and still in the same clothes. Elsie wanted to go home to shower and change, so I drove her in the old van to the top of the town and came back. The pub was still in darkness, but I heard Colin get up a minute or two after I got in. He had to prepare breakfast for the agronomists

I went downstairs to offer a hand.

"How much did you drink last night?" he asked. "You look awful."

"I'll probably wake up in a while," I said.

"Don't worry, I can cope," he said.

I went back and made myself a coffee at the machine and sat on a bar stool to drink it. Elsie's figurine was still on the counter. I smiled. Next to it I noticed for the first time a long, narrow parcel, wrapped in brown paper. An envelope was Sellotaped to the parcel. I opened the envelope and pulled out a small card, signed by Mike and the other four workers. It wished me a happy birthday. I tore open the parcel. It was a piece of oak which had been smoothed and polished like silk and my name had been printed in gold on the polished wood. I was suitably touched and placed the piece on the bar.

There are many kinds of love, I was discovering. Until that time, I had not experienced much of any sort. Now I was undergoing a big step in my emotional education. As a teenager, twelve years previously, I had fallen in love. At the time we both thought we had found the secret of life, and for a few months we enjoyed that passionate experience, believing we held the future between us, that we could overcome all obstacles. It lasted less than a year. Since then, I had had a few, casual liaisons which were all about lust, not love. I hardly knew my father. My mother treated me more like a schoolboy in need of supervision than her own flesh and blood. At the age of fifteen I entered the disciplined, adult world of work, while my brother and sister remained at school. We saw little of one another. So, at the age of 33, I had little experience of love of any kind. I realised that Elsie offered unquestioning friendship to begin with. That friendship would surely develop into something else, something I had never known before. We found time somehow to talk in the days and weeks that followed. Once, I suggested that people who felt as we did usually got married.

"No," Elsie said. "I don't want to marry. It's not that I'm scared of the commitment, Tom. We are two independent people. We love one another and we shall almost certainly be happy together the rest of our lives, but I shall never *belong* to you, nor you to me. "

I understood where she was coming from. Each of us had a life to lead for ourselves, part of which was better done alone. Elsie loved her work as I loved mine. We were able and willing to discuss our individual interests, but neither of us wanted to run the other's life. Our love burned deep and strong and was unshakeable. Kitty was close to both of us. It would be a while before she found a similar relationship with Colin. I came to understand or at least to recognise her loving friendship. I was also privileged to enjoy with the Famous Five, a title I began to use, a kindness which was a kind of love too. These different kinds of love helped us work together, usually in harmony.

 The weeks and months passed. Goosemere felt like a vast building site. Now the road was always muddy, not the black mud of the Gann, but a grey, clay-like mud that got everywhere. We were constantly washing and scrubbing floors. The South Wing fared worst as the agronomists came every evening with mud on their boots, The minibus brought more mud on the cobbles. The top of the town suffered less, and it felt as though I was escaping whenever I took a trip up the hill. The Famous Five complained about it. They were further inconvenienced by having to avoid bringing mud into the East Wing when coming from their workroom. Everyone looked forward to the day when we could escape the mud. It was to take three years. It affected adversely the mood of the town, especially our end. I kept reminding myself that once the redevelopment was finished, things would improve. We would be in the topographical centre of the remodelled town.

Meanwhile, it was clear that we were adversely affected by the building of the new houses. After speaking to Colin, I phoned John Stanwyck and said I was getting worried.

"Time for a rethink," he said, and said he would pay us a visit.

He came three days later and saw the mess for himself. He had already looked at the figures we had sent him.

"It looks as though you are back to living on an overdraft," he said. "And I can't now see that things are going to get much easier for a while. To be positive, the long term looks good. There are two elements in your plan which are not yet fully operable. The first is the use of your rooms to accommodate hotel guests. I know you're famous five workers have been doing a fine job, but they have only completed two rooms, as I understand it."

"Yes, that's right. It's a slow business. There's no point in doing a skimpy job. We did that with the South Wing, and it worked, but we need to attract guests who will pay more."

"The second string to your bow," John went on, "is to be a proper restaurant. With the right refurbishment, it must surely be close to the time when it would work."

"Maybe," Colin agreed, "but I'm not sure that the bar is the best place for the kind of service we had in mind."

"I'm afraid," John said, "my view is that you need more investment. I realise you do not have the ready money, so the answer must be to look for more funding. I've done a bit of thinking. The income from the sale of the West Wing certainly helped a lot, even after tax. Thank you by the way for paying my invoice. I've knocked up another, rough plan. You may be unwilling to accept it. It will mean more debt for a while, that's the way investment works, I'm afraid. I'm sure, in view of your history, the bank would look kindly on it."

He handed both of us a copy of his plan. It involved seeking an even bigger overdraft and would, I was sure, leave us facing months or even years of anxiety, uncertainty, the very problems I had experienced before.

"Can you really think," Colin asked, "the bank would lend us all this money?"

"We shall never know unless we ask," John said, "but I think they will. As your financial adviser, I believe your long-term business plan is very sound. It's just that it is still too early. The redevelopment that's going on has obviously affected you financially, but ultimately it will benefit you, especially since the Harbour Lights is now much more central to the town itself. You must not forget, either, that the Community Centre will attract not only local people, but visitors and the Centre is part of your premises."

"I'm not sure," I said, "that I can endure the worry of dealing with such a huge debt again. This is even bigger than the last overdraft."

"It needs to be, Tom," John said. "But I can understand your hesitation. What I'm recommending is a total refurbishment of both the South and the East Wing. I am not an architect, of course. I can't say how much it would cost. If the idea interests you at all, I suggest you consult an architect to get some idea of cost and practicality. There would be no point in going to see a bank manager without that kind of information."

The new plan was indeed something on a grand scale. Both the South and East Wings were to be renovated. The bar area was to be made smaller, allowing for a separate, newly designed dining room. The hallway at the south end of the East Wing was to be converted to provide a proper, if small, office. Upstairs in the East Wing, the private accommodation occupied by me and by Kitty and Colin was to move to the top floor. This would allow the whole of the first floor to be used as guest rooms. Since two of these had already been converted, it would be a little less bother to finish the rest.

John left us to think about it and returned home. I lay awake all night and again, the old anxiety returning. I told Colin how I felt. He understood. He was almost aghast at the size of the potential debt. We tried to put that to one side and looked at the forecast John had made of future income and expenditure if we were to pursue the new plan. John had never let me down so far.

"I suppose," I said, "we have nothing much to lose by consulting an architect, except for his fee."

"I have no idea what kind of fees they charge," Colin admitted.

"Probably big ones," I said gloomily.

I asked Kitty to look for architectural firms who might undertake planning.

"What are you planning now?" she asked.

"Just following up an idea of John's," I said.

In next to no time, she came back to me with the names of four local architects I looked at their websites. One of them specialised in schools. Another built houses. One, who looked the most likely, had a very mixed portfolio which included conversions of older properties. One such conversion had been of a former, Victorian factory into luxury flats. I contacted him. His name was Vernon Washington.

A few days later Vernon paid us a visit. He had with him a young, female assistant whose primary job seem to be to feed information into her iPad. I took them into a quiet area of the bar where, together with Colin, I tried to explain the situation. I described John's suggestions. He asked if I had plans of the existing buildings. I found those which my father had obtained when we first bought the Harbour Lights

"These will do for now," Vernon said, "but I shall need to redraw them accurately."

The four of us trooped through the South Wing to start with. And Vernon and his assistant used a laser to take note of the exact measurements of each room. Vernon was particularly interested in the outside doorways and the staircases. We moved back to the bar and through to the kitchen and the fish and chip shop. He made few comments, except to ask questions about such banal matters as the whereabouts of stopcocks, the electricity and gas supply, the certificates, including the Fire Certificate. He was meticulous about measuring the large bar area, noting that part of it had been arranged as somewhere people could eat. He checked out the two staircases, saw that there were just three occupied rooms on the first floor on one side of a partition. On the other side, the Five were at work. They had completed the basic refurbishment of just two rooms. He looked at that. Mike and his fellow-workers said nothing but watched with interest. Then we climbed the staircase to the top floor. Here the rooms were largely untouched, except for some of the decorating materials which the Five had brought across from the South Wing. I explained what we had been doing to date.

"How radical are you prepared for me to be, if I design some new plans?"

"I'm not sure what you mean by radical," I said. "Obviously, I would need to work within a budget, but, if I like what you suggest, I shall need to secure suitable funding."

"Right, then. I like the look of the place," Vernon said. "But, if you really want to turn it into a practical business, combining three separate elements, you probably need to make some radical, major changes to the layout."

"How major?"

"Let me have a good look and draw up some plans," he said. "I rather think everything is the wrong way round. If you want to run both an hotel and a restaurant, you'd be best advised to keep the businesses physically separate. Hotel guests may want to use the restaurant of course, but they won't want to gain access to their rooms through a bar, as now. Furthermore, the occupied rooms on the first floor of this wing are in the prime position and, I assume they are used by your staff – yourself, maybe?"

"Yes, they happened to be the first rooms we renovated."

"At present, guests would have to come here through a public bar and use the same staircase as the staff. Leave me to look at it."

They left.

"What do you think?" I asked Colin.

"I think we are going to be facing a big bill," he said. I laughed, but I thought much the same.

The plans, when they arrived by courier some weeks later, were fascinating. We were both desperate to look at them, but we did not want the Famous Five to see them until we had decided what our next step would be. We got together in the kitchen, not wanting to deal with questions from Kitty either.

We were not merely surprised by Vernon's ideas; we were thoroughly shocked. Work which had already been done or begun would be thrown out. The kitchen would be almost the only part of the East Wing that would be unchanged. The staircases would be left in the same places, but even they would be changed to allow different access. The one at the south end of the East Wing. Was to undergo a major (and horrendously expensive) change. Vernon proposed to join the two parts of the building to make a largely glass entrance tower, encasing the stairs, but adding a lift. The rest of both wings would be completely gutted, and the South Wing would house the hotel reception. The entire South Wing would now look outwards, and the main entrance would be at the corner where the new lobby was planned. Vernon even recommended that the flagged floors should be levelled, and doorways widened to allow wheelchair access. The South Wing, he recommended, should be renovated first, allowing us to open eight double rooms plus two on the ground floor. In the East Wing the Dining Room would be moved to where the existing bar was, and a smaller bar with a separate entrance would be in the middle of the ground floor, but partition walls would allow guests to access the Dining Room without entering the new bar. Rooms occupied by me, Colin and Kitty, including her office, would still be on the first floor, but there would be a functioning office as part of the new Reception.

"What will all this cost?" Colin asked.

"And how long would we be forced to shut?"

Without asking a few builders we could not know, but it looked beyond us. A big question was where the guests would come from in this small but growing town. Our uncertainty was compounded at the same time by the growth of the new estate. Several of the agronomists had put down deposits on new houses. They were eager to move in the coming months to their own properties, close to the Agronomy Station.

The one-bedroomed accommodation in the South Wing would soon be redundant.

It was time to put Kitty in the picture. Her skills were needed to find builders who might quote us a price. Inevitably, Elsie asked questions. We swore her to secrecy (not strictly necessary; she would not have discussed our business anyway) but her local knowledge, the rest of us agreed, might prove useful. I was far from sure we were even looking in the right direction. I could feel fear at times causing my heart to flutter. We addressed five bids in all. They varied enormously, though we knew different materials and finishes would vary. All five estimates made us gasp.

Yet again we faced difficult choices, but this time I was not on my own. After my heart to heart with Elsie on the night of my birthday, I was aware how I had changed. I was no longer hell-bent on doing everything myself. I was thankful to take decisions as part of this small group. But this was a very big decision. Were we being far too ambitious? It was time for more detailed advice from John Stanwyck.

Before we could set up such a meeting, events took an unexpected turn. My father had now been charged with fraud and remanded in custody. The trial would take place a year later. Meanwhile, two deaths occurred in one week. The first was Chris, the plasterer. He was rushed into hospital with a pulmonary embolism and died within hours. The other four were devastated. They had worked together, played together, sang together, and laughed together. Five men who defeated the loneliness that came from bereavement and isolation by banding together.

"We need time to get over this," said Mike. "We won't be able to carry on with your rooms for a bit. I hope you'll understand."

"Of course, I understand, Mike, to tell you the truth, we're having to decide a lot of things now. We may have to make some radical changes."

"What does that mean?" he asked.

"We've got to rethink the business," I said, not wanting to tell him too much. "All that work you put into the South Wing looks like being less important now the Agronomy Station is getting established."

"I see that," he said. "Are you going to re-do all those rooms? I'm not sure the four of us would want to tackle that again."

"You did a great job, thank you." The subject changed to the coming funeral.

But the day before Chris's funeral, I was in the bar, serving coffees to a group of Elsie's friends when Kitty came downstairs. One look at her face told me there was bad news.

"It's Mum," she said." Mrs Goodhew found her this morning when she arrived to do the cleaning. She was sitting in her favourite chair and the dogs were prowling round, making whining noises. She died there, all alone."

Kitty had got on well with her mother. She was clearly very upset. Tony had phoned her first. He rang me later, he said, because I had never seemed to be close. He was quite right, but my feelings were strangely mixed. Maybe I had nursed a secret and forlorn hope that one day I could relate to my mother in a more normal way. It would never happen now. Was it my fault somehow? I felt real regret. I had never come to understand this woman who had carried me in her body for nine months, but who had treated me consistently with coldness. My duty, I now felt, was to support both Kitty and Tony.

I explained to Colin and asked if he could cope for a few days if I went home with Kitty. It could be a couple of weeks. This was a slack time. Routines were in place. Colin had my phone number for emergencies. I trusted him. I also rang Elsie to explain. She came immediately to spend time with Kitty. I tidied up one or two bits of e-mail correspondence, packed a bag, and was ready to drive in Kitty's car back to the family home to meet Tony.

Chapter seven

Anyone who has had to sort out the house of a parent after their death will understand how dreadful a task it is. The three of us shared the chore. We slept in our old bedrooms, but that brought strange memories which differed between me and my siblings. I had been mostly solitary as a child, conscious of the different ways we were treated. I was often jealous of both Tony and Kitty, and they clung more closely together. As a teenager, I was working from the age of fifteen and saw them only when I came home in the evenings. Later, as they progressed through schools and eventually university, they were experiencing things I knew nothing about. I was learning how to prepare and serve meals, or the legal requirements imposed on hotel owners. I knew about dealing with members of the public, about keeping your private opinions and feelings to yourself. Now I was a man in a boy's bedroom. I could see how Kitty and Tony were affected by a grief I could not fully share, but the job of sorting and clearing felt like the physical dismantling of a life. From time to time, either of them would come across some apparently meaningless object which became a sharp reminder of the past. Kitty cried a great deal. Tony's face seemed permanently strained. I felt nothing, or very little, then felt guilty at my lack of emotion.

I took over the arrangements for the funeral. The dogs were collected by a local charity who, we understood, had already been asked well in advance to care for them if she were to die. I registered the death. I had to ask Kitty to make a list of mourners. She tried, but soon found my mother had virtually no friends. We asked her cleaner; she excused herself. In the event there were the undertakers, us and our father, complete with a discreet escort. The service was conducted by the local vicar who, as became clear when he called to discuss the service, had never known my mother. We stood in the rain to watch the coffin disappear in the grave. It was all very sad, but the sadness in my case was not from a sense of personal loss so much as the lack of meaning in a life so lived.

We had a little time with our father. Kitty hugged him. She would forgive him anything. Tony was more circumspect, treating him with politeness and avoiding confrontation. I treated my father with the same, cold courtesy that his wife had shown me. He asked awkwardly how the Harbour Lights project was going. I told him it was OK. With so few to mourn her, we had not bothered with a reception of any kind. My father and his escort left and we went back to the house. My mood matched the surroundings. The house was not empty, but it felt empty. I poured whiskies for the three of us.

"Kitty," I said, "one of us should begin sorting the contents of Mum's desk. Do you want me or Tony to do it? It will be upsetting, looking into her private papers.

"No," she said, "I'll do it, but I may need to ask you, if I don't understand something."

We had always been told, when she was alive, that the desk was her very private property, that none of us should touch it, so it was now a difficult task.

Kitty unlocked the bureau as though it contained a bomb. It was neatly organised. An old-fashioned blotter lay on the writing surface. There was only a cheque book on top. I was interested in the bank she used. I had never heard of it. The address in the cheque book was in Guernsey. A paying-in book had a similar bank, but only one cheque had been paid in. The receipt slip was stamped by a local branch of a High Street bank.

Tentatively, Kitty emptied one of the small pigeonholes. It contained several items of differing sizes. One, official-looking document was folded in three and tied in a red ribbon.

"Oh!" Kitty exclaimed," It's a will. Should we be reading this?"

"We need to," I said, "if only to find out who the executor is."

"I don't like reading it," Kitty said. "It's so personal."

Even Tony found this strange. He looked at me over his glass and raised his eyebrows.

"Pass it over," I said.

The Executor's name was given in the first clause. It was a solicitor, and his office was in the nearby town. We would have to contact him in the morning, I said, meanwhile we should acquaint ourselves with the contents. They were likely to concern us as her heirs. I began to read the pedantic, legalistic language.

On her death, after taxes and expenses had been paid, the house and contents were to be sold. One third of the estate was then to go to a local animal charity.

"One third! That is a huge amount of money!" exclaimed Tony. "Whatever else he did, Dad knew all about the property market. I don't know what he paid for it, but what do you think it's worth now" He was looking at me.

"Don't forget there will be things like death duty and Capital Gains," I said. "At a guess, I'd say between one point two and one point six million."

Kitty gasped.

"Read on, Tom," Tony said.

"It gets complicated here," I said. "I hope your maths is up to it."

Having disposed of one third of the estate to charity, the will required the two-thirds that were left to be divided in five. Both Tony and Kitty were baffled, thinking I had misread it for 'into three'. No, the five parts would now go to the three of us, Tony and Kitty each to receive two fifths, myself to receive one fifth. They were both indignant on my behalf. Tony even suggested I should make a legal challenge. That, as I saw it, would make for ugly quarrels, even among lawyers, who would also take their fees.

With the aid of Kitty's iPad, we played with some figures. I suggested the estate, not including the contents, which might pay at least some of the legal fees, including the executor's commission, at an optimistic, one point five million. The money left after the dogs had their large share would then be one million. The threshold, or tax- free element, was £325,000, leaving £675,000 on which Inheritance tax would be due at the reduced rate of 32%. It would have been 40% but more than 10% of the full estate had been given to charity. The amount to be shared would then be a total of about £685K. By now Kitty looked lost. She wanted only the bottom line.

"Of course," I pointed out, "it all depends on what the house and garden sell for, but, if it was the one and a half million, we suggested, you two would receive about £274K each. I would get half that, say £137K."

"That's less than one tenth of the value!" Tony pointed out.

"Yes, the Government would take more than my share."

The silence that followed felt quite gloomy. We were all ruminating on the unfairness.

"You can understand how families can be affected by things like this," Kitty said. "I suppose we should all be thinking Mum has left us sizeable sums. Before this, I've been content when my bank balance has been more than a hundred pounds at the end of the month."

She turned back to the bureau and pulled out a handful of yellowing papers. She examined them one by one. They appeared to be mementos – old tickets, receipts from hotels she had used, a few photographs, a folded newspaper clipping. When she unfolded it, it was a report in a local paper of a wedding. The caption named Mr Jack Hammond, Miss Rosemary Fairbanks, the bride, and Miss Emily Fairbanks, bridesmaid, sister of the bride.

"I never knew she had a sister," I said. Nor did Tony or Kitty.

"We have an aunt!" Kitty said, excited.

"Hold on," Tony pointed out, "this was over thirty years ago. We don't even know if she's still alive. If she is, why hasn't she been around?"

Kitty was determined to find out more about our Aunt Emily. She had a researcher's expertise and determination. She found the marriage certificate and discovered the Registry Office where our parents had married. Next, she searched for Emily Fairbanks. It was highly likely she had married and so changed her name, but Kitty was lucky. In the Register of voters, the name appeared. A Miss Emily Fairbanks was a permanent resident in a sheltered housing complex only fifteen miles away. Kitty rang the Warden, who was suspicious at first, then said she would speak to Miss Fairbanks. A few hours later, the Warden rang back to say Miss Fairbanks would see us.

Aunt Emily's sitting room was small. It was not designed to take more than one guest at a time. We squeezed in. We did not know what to expect, but we were pleasantly surprised to find a sharp-witted, grey-haired old lady with a twinkle in her eye.

"Well, now," she said. "This is a wonderful surprise. I suppose you," pointing at me, "must be Tom. Am I right?"

"Yes, I'm Tom," I said. "Forgive us if we don't know you. None of us can remember ever seeing you before."

"No, and it's mostly down to me, I'm afraid. I – I more or less cut myself off from the family. I have sometimes regretted it, as now."

"What do you mean?" Kitty asked. "Cut yourself off? Why?"

Aunt Emily sighed. "I suppose I have always feared that this moment would come when I would have to explain myself. Has your mother not told you anything about us?"

Suddenly it occurred to me that she did not know that her sister had died. I was not sure how to tell her. Fortunately, she seemed preoccupied with her own thoughts.

"I wonder if I could ask you, dear," she said to Kitty, "if you would mind making some tea for us. Everything is on the table there."

"Miss Fairbanks – or should I call you Aunt Emily? – there is so much we must tell you," I said. "You seem to know me, Tom, but do you know my brother and sister, Tony and Kitty?"

"I guessed. I feel dreadful never to have met you before. It sounds like a cliché, but the last time I saw you, Tom, you were an infant, just over a year old."

"Let me begin with the bad news," I said. "The reason we are all together, and the reason that we have found you is that our mother died three weeks ago. We found a picture of you among her belongings. Otherwise, we didn't know that you existed."

"Dead? Oh dear! Now I feel even worse than before. I should have put things straight. Now it's too late."

Kitty poured four cups of tea in pretty, delicate porcelain cups. They were handed round solemnly, like a ritual.

"It's too late to put things straight with your mother," said Aunt Emily, "but at least I can try to explain to you. I am so sorry to have missed your childhood. I don't even know what you now do."

Tony explained.

"I'm glad you are all doing well," she said. "I only wish I had been there to see you grow up or, in the case of you, Kitty and you, Tony, I didn't even know you existed, any more than you knew about me. Perhaps I'd better start at the beginning. The story goes right back to the wedding you mentioned. I'm afraid I never liked your father, Jack. All those years ago, I thought there was something about him – well, let's say I didn't trust him. Perhaps, if he had been more supportive and approachable, some of the disaster might have been avoided."

We were listening avidly but baffled. What disaster?

"Your mother, my sister, Rosemary, became pregnant almost immediately. Jack, who was in the building trade, I think, seemed to spend a great deal of time away from home, leaving your mother in a small, terraced house for weeks on end sometimes. Of course, I kept her company whenever I could, but I was working, so she had a lonely time of it. Her only companion for much of the time was a cat. As the months passed, she was more and more uncomfortable. I don't know where the midwife came from, but she was dreadful, she showed virtually no sympathy at all. Your father was away when your poor mother went into labour with you, Tom. It was a bad labour. She was in a great deal of pain for three whole days, and the wretched midwife insisted that this must be a natural birth and pain relief was not a good idea. By the end of the second night in agony, poor Rosemary was utterly exhausted, and the doctor, when he was finally summoned, was shocked at the damage you had caused by your delayed entry into the world. When you finally made your appearance, Tom, your mother did not want to know you. She refused even to touch you, told everyone to take you away, said   she never wanted to see you. I understand that initial rejection often seems to happen, but as the weeks passed the problem did not go away. Jack came home but showed little patience. Rosemary suffered severe postnatal depression. It was so severe that she threatened to kill herself. In the end, she was taken into a mental hospital for her own protection. I tried to help with your care, but your father was obliged to hire a nurse for nearly a year."

All three of us found this very affecting. It began to explain my mother's coldness towards me. I had, indeed, caused her a great deal of pain, both physical and mental.

"She must have recovered," I said. "After all, she came home, and she gave birth to these two," pointing at my brother and sister.

"Well, it was more complicated than that. When she came home from Hospital, she was still cold towards you. I'm afraid she never, to my knowledge, managed to forge that mother-son bond all the time I knew her. But she had had nothing to do with you for a full year. In fact, she was so cold towards you, even when she was supposed to be back to normal, that I was very concerned for you. I told her what I thought. She brushed off my criticism time and time again, and then came the day when I lost control of myself, I'm afraid. We ended up having a truly violent row. Remember, I had been having this strong argument for months. This time we had come to the end. She told me I was no

longer welcome, that she did not want to see me ever again. I am ashamed to say that I said the same to her. I washed my hands of her. I kept my word, and I never saw her again."

She looked very sad. It was as though she had shrunk. Kitty instinctively knelt by her chair and put an arm around her thin shoulders.

It was a sad story, but for the first time I began to understand. I don't think I was quite ready to forgive my mother for all those years of coldness, but it helped to understand how they had occurred.

193

Aunt Emily perked up, asked for another cup of tea, and asked us in more detail what we had done with our lives. She was glad that I had survived such a childhood and had become a successful hotelier. She was delighted that Tony had progressed to become the head of his own school. She was very impressed by Kitty's technical expertise. The afternoon passed happily, and we all promised to return in the future.

We drove back home without speaking much. We all loved this little old woman and were really pleased we had tracked her down. In my own case, she had solved a mystery which had dogged me all my life.

Chapter eight

Kitty and I returned to Goosemere, and Tony went back to Megan. She was expecting their second child, so had not come to the funeral. Tony had managed to spend a couple of days with her, leaving us in the old house, but he was plainly glad to get home. The house was now in the hands of an estate agent. The executor was busy following the instructions in my mother's will. We had not much more we could do.

Colin was pleased to see us and we him. There was still plenty of mud everywhere. The houses on the estate were multiplying at an astonishing rate. They were timber framed, built partly in the factory and brought on the backs of lorries to be erected on concrete foundations. In a very short time, the muddy service road was lined with houses on either side and began to look almost tidy. Further streets were to lead off this first one. Several of the finished houses were already occupied by people who worked on the Agronomy Station

The Harbour Lights was once more in financial decline. The South Wing was now almost half empty. The mud, which in dry weather became a fine, grey powder, blown in the prevailing, easterly winds, made everything miserable. It was not entirely surprising that our bar takings were also down. I personally missed the Famous Five, their numbers now reduced to four. One or other of them called in from time to time for a drink, but it was not the same as having them on the premises daily, sometimes singing cheerily as they worked. Mike came to perch on a bar stool to drink a pint of beer, looking and sounding like just another customer I told him that trade was poor, and that Colin and I were considering radical changes.

"Needs must when the Devil drives," he observed. "I think you're right. This town is changing. If you're going to make this place work, you'll have to change with it." I suppose he was grieving for Chris. The ironic humour had all but disappeared and he looked older.

I asked if the remaining four planned to resume working on their original boat-building project.

"We have lost interest, to tell the truth. We thought, maybe, when the new Centre is ready, we might use that, but it doesn't look as if there will be a suitable space there. Maybe it's time we called it a day. We're old men. Time to stop."

It made me quite sad to see the change in him. The other three, when I saw them, were equally despondent. I told Elsie.

"That's really sad," she said. "It sounds as though they are giving up on life, not just their boat."

"The boat was only an excuse to meet regularly."

"I have an idea," she said, but she wouldn't say more.

I asked John Stanwyck to come down and talk to us, help us make up our minds about Vernon Washington's plans-. I was still worried. The reconstruction which Vernon had suggested was extremely expensive. Could we recoup such a huge outlay? The town was growing, that was obvious, but would there be demand enough to support a new hotel? After all, it is not the residents in a town that need hotel accommodation. What was there in Goosemere to attract visitors?

If we did not go ahead with further investment and change, what then, I asked. The signs were that the Harbour Lights would continue to dim and soon might go out altogether. The business, in whatever shape, was valid only as part of the community, like the new Centre. With Colin's agreement I invited both Kitty and Elsie to this consultation. Neither of them, of course, had the right to make any decisions, but I felt their comments and interested input would help us come to a balanced view of the future. So, five of us sat around the table, having closed the bar for two hours.

"I often feel," I confessed, "that this place is like an albatross around my neck. No sooner do we deal with one crisis than n another comes along."

"I understand how you feel," John said. "And I'm not sure that my advice is especially helpful. The thing is, ultimately, the decision you must make is a matter of faith. None of us can be absolutely certain the Harbour Lights has a future as a high -quality hotel. That will depend entirely on whether there is sufficient demand, and, yet we cannot really tell."

"Perhaps," Elsie joined in, "you use the right word, faith. I know I can't make up your mind for you, either of you, and I am biased. I believe Goosemere still has a future. I'm not entirely sure what kind of future, but I feel it is going to be an improvement. The Council obviously thinks the same way, or they would not have produced the plan, nor would the Government have put money into the grant we are using. You just had to believe, as I do, that they are right."

"That's all very well," I said, "but you can't live on faith. We need to earn money. We can only do that if people in sufficient numbers want to come and stay here. Meanwhile, we are gradually going to run out of cash again."

Colin spoke for the first time. "When you asked me to come and help you, Tom," he said, "I came because I believed not so much in Goosemere and the County Council, but because I believed in you. I know you wanted to build a kind of empire here and that it proved much more difficult than you thought, but you have survived, I'm not sure how. The collapse of Cornblend, anyone would have thought, should have been the end. I joined you, hoping we might one day be running a decent hotel and a more than decent restaurant. I still think we could."

"That's kind of you, Colin. I've already told you how much your help and very hard work mean to me. You still haven't got your restaurant."

"Well," John said, "all that is fine and dandy and embarrassingly touchy-feely. You have both put a lot of work into this place. As co-directors, it's up to you to decide one way or another what to do next. Your choices, as I see them, are to do nothing, to make one or two minor changes and hope they will boost trade sufficiently to make you profitable again, or to bite the bullet and borrow a huge amount of money."

"What does 'a huge amount of money mean?" Kitty asked.

"The scheme proposed by Vernon Washington is on a grand scale," John said. "It would transform this place, turn it into a first -rate establishment, with about 16 or 18 letting bedrooms as well as a good restaurant. It also allows for the fish and chip shop to continue, and that has always been profitable. The bar, although smaller, is never likely to lose money. The trouble is that, to do all the building work suggested by Vernon would cost an estimated half million. The interest on a loan of that size might negate the value of the potential increase in income.

We cannot be sure of such an increase, but the new Agronomy Station may well attract visitors."

"Don't forget the effects of the new Community Centre," Elsie pointed out. "We are hoping that we shall attract several kinds of visitors, especially if we can run special courses in this, that and the other. Gus Carter is already planning to expand his work. There will also be a few professional people who need to visit the new school, and the other businesses in the new estates. The Council is planning to make the riverside more attractive in simple but effective ways. For example, they are planning to erect fencing along the river and past the Cymbeline as far as a hide for birdwatchers. They will provide a pleasant kind of promenade. We have suggested that a simple signpost should be erected at the new crossroads, pointing out things like the new Centre, the hotel, the Cymbeline, the Agronomy Station and so on."

"Did you say half a million pounds?" Kitty asked.

"About that."

It still looked an impossibly large sum to borrow. Our overdraft at this time stood at 200 K.

"I have a proposal to put to you, then."

All eyes were now on Kitty.

"You all know that our mother died a very short time ago," she said. "The old home, where she lived, is in a fast -developing part of the Home Counties. We have just been told of the most recent valuation. It is even bigger than we had imagined. We also have been told that there is stiff competition to buy it. Of course, we shall have to wait for probate, which is likely to take a few months, but my brothers and I will inherit a lot of money." I looked at her, guessing what she was going to say next. I was right.

"Between us, Tom and I will inherit over half the equity. That will not be half a million, but it will be more than a quarter of a million"

"Kitty," I said," you can't give all that money to me."

"That is not exactly what I am proposing," she said. "What I am proposing is that I buy into your business, become a third director. I wouldn't want to use my entire inheritance that way, I want to keep a little for myself, but I could offer most of it. I am not going to speak for Tony, who is not here, and any way he has other commitments. I believe he is planning to buy a house with his inheritance. At present, he has accommodation provided by the school where he is headmaster, but he needs his own property"

"Kitty," I said, "are you sure? It's going to be a huge risk."

"If you believe in it, and if Colin believes in you, I'd like to go ahead."

Nobody spoke for a moment, taking in the enormity of the gamble that Kitty was taking. Colin looked torn. Such an investment would give us a sporting chance, but it could be at a huge cost to Kitty herself.

"Well," John said, "it would certainly solve the immediate problem. It would enable you to commission a builder to make a start on the changes that Vernon proposes. You would need to borrow, I suggest, something like £200,000 just to be safe. That would be manageable. You may need less. But you now have two decisions to make. Are you prepared to accept Kitty's offer? Are you prepared to invest in a new hotel?"

"I think this is something only Colin and I can decide between us," I said "I must say, Kitty, that I am very concerned about accepting your offer. It's a great deal of money which you could probably invest far more securely just by speaking to a stockbroker. If we accept, we shall have to contact Roland to reorganise our company. I'm not sure if I would even remain the principal shareholder."

"I rather think you would," said John.

Probate took a further six months. The value of the estate proved to be just under two million, a considerable increase on the amount we had suggested. When the funds were released, the executor calculated our shares as £181,000 for me and £360,000 for each of the others. None of us had ever had this kind of money before. It made me doubly nervous. I was happy to put nearly all of my money into the business, but I insisted that Kitty's share should be limited to a quarter of a million. Even so, that got us within comfortable, striking distance of the amount needed. Negotiations inevitably took a long time. Articles of Association were rewritten, and Kitty became a full director. We continued to survive, although our income was diminishing. At last, everything was in place, contracts signed, and a start date agreed. A whole year had gone by since my mother's funeral.

Kitty, Colin and I sat in the bar one evening after closing time with a nightcap.

"You realise," I pointed out, "that in two weeks' time, when the builders move in, we shall all have to move out? What are you both going to do?"

They had given it a little thought. Kitty had arranged for her precious equipment to be moved into storage, while she intended to go with Colin to visit his parents in Pembrokeshire. It was about time, Kitty explained, that she met her intended parents-in-law. I was unaware that Colin had proposed, but I was delighted for them.

"Have you got any plans?" Kitty asked.

"Only sketchy ones," I said. "Elsie is happy for me to move in with her for a short time, but, frankly, there is very little space and I think we might begin to annoy one another if I stayed too long. I fancy going away for a week or two, letting the builders get on with it. I think I would find the whole thing very stressful, if I were to stay. It is going to be very noisy and uncomfortable, especially at the beginning, when they are digging up the flag stones and lay new floors. All any of us could do would be to stand outside and watch. I don't really fancy that, not in the least."

"I imagine," said Colin, "that the rebuild of the corner of the South Wing could be even worse. They are going to have to take part of the walls down. It will look horrible to begin with. Thank God they're not going to touch the kitchen."

"How long do they reckon it will take?" Kitty asked, "Six months? That sounds very quick."

"No," Colin corrected her, "six months is only to complete the shell of the place. There will still be all the interior fittings and fixtures and decorating to be done."

We sat in silence, daunted by the prospect. It was going to be difficult in effect to be without a home for six months. Colin explained that he wanted to take advantage of the time to work with a well-known chef who had a successful restaurant in the Cotswolds. That, at least, was a constructive use of his time. I did not want to be away from Elsie for too long, but I would have to find new accommodation.

Elsie was happy for me to stay for the first two weeks, but she agreed it would be better for both of us if I could find somewhere else after that. She was not being inhospitable, merely sensible, and I knew it. Had we been able to live together in the hotel, things would have been easier and less crowded, perhaps. However, Elsie turned up with an unexpected suggestion on the second day.

"You know," she said, "I was at a committee meeting today?" I nodded. "Well, of course Gus Carter was there. He has a problem of his own, so I volunteered you to solve it for him."

"What kind of problem?" I was suspicious.

"He is due to take the Cymbeline downriver tomorrow. He needs a crew of twelve, but one of them has had to go home suddenly. So," she said gaily, "I said he would step in."

"You what?"

"Oh, come on, Tom, you'll enjoy it. You'll get board and lodging, plenty of fresh air and exercise, and you will be out of my hair."

"I thought you liked having me around."

"You know I do, but I have been neglecting my own business for a while. I am running low on basic stocks. I need to make a new batch of cups, mugs, all that sort of thing. I need to spend probably four or five days up to my elbows in clay. I shall be exhausted every evening. Once all that stuff has been dried out, I shall need to load the kiln. I should be much happier, knowing that you were enjoying yourself somewhere else."

"If you put it like that," I said, "it's hard to say no. But what will I be expected to do?"

"From my experience – and I have only been on one of these trips – it will involve a great deal of hauling in sheets."

"Sheets? You're not volunteering me to do the laundry, surely?"

She laughed. I still loved that sound. "Ropes," she said. "Sheets are what the ropes are called. Oh dear! You are going to learn a great deal, I imagine. It will do you no end of good, and you're going to be so tired you won't have time to worry about the Harbour Lights."

She was right about that. Gus was pleased to see me. He was too busy to say much, except, "Good for Louise!" and he introduced me to my fellow, eleven greenhorns. They were all much younger than me, but we got along fine.

It was, indeed, an interesting and novel experience. Gus was a master mariner, so we were in good hands. The work was quite hard, but it was shared, and it was good for me. I slept like a log in my narrow bunk.

I was accepted by the youngsters, although they were uncertain to begin with.

We sailed down the river on the flood tide and out to sea.

I learned a few nautical terms in the process. I had noticed the leeboards while the Cymbeline was sitting on the mud. I had thought they were simply there like elbows, to prop her up, and stop her from leaning one way or the other. It was when we reached the sea, that their true purpose became clear. These barges were flat bottomed and, having no keel, their massive sails would naturally capsize them. The leeboards served as a keel, enabling the big craft to cope comfortably at sea as well as in the river. I learned too that the huge mast could be lowered, enabling the barge to pass under bridges. The bottom of the mast was housed in a large, wooden, boxlike structure, called a tabernacle. I learned that in their heyday these massive vessels were manned by just two men. To help them manoeuvre, especially in port, the mainsail was often lowered, and it was the topsail that was used. As soon as the skipper wanted to give way, to take some of the momentum off, the topsail could be collapsed immediately by 'letting go' one rope, or halyard. These magnificent barges were in common use until the middle of the 19th century. This trip, which took us as far as the Medway, was like going back in time. I enjoyed it far more than I expected.

Gus asked me to stay on board when the other eleven had disembarked. Now that the Cymbeline was safely moored, he could afford to chat. He was a fascinating man has, I suppose, most mariners or ex-mariners are. He had travelled all over the world. Once he settled in Goosemere, he had come to love the town. He was also very fond of Louise, as he called her. During his career, he had made a little money, which he now supplemented by running his week-long courses. I remembered that he had given £1000 to the Community Fund. He was also a member of the committee. At the last meeting, he said, Louise had talked to him about the four-man who wanted to run a "men's shed". There was not a great deal of space in the new Centre, but Gus was taken by the idea. Elsie had put him in touch with Mike.

The two men were of an age. Their experience, their skills were different, but they both had a need to be active. In Mike's case, and in that of the other three members of the Shed, the enthusiasm had waned after the death of Chris. Gus asked if he could see the boat they had been working on in Archie's garage. The Four were happy to show him. In fact, they discovered their interest was reawakened once it had been observed by an interested outsider. For his part, Gus was impressed by the quality of the workmanship. The plan which they were using was a design for a traditional, open boat. The Four, as they showed him the work they had done so far, were keen to explain. The garage was still called, not a convenient place to be using for a workshop.

"I understand there aren't any spaces big enough for this in the new Centre," Gus said.

"No," said Archie. "We are all too old and creaky these days to go on working here for hours at a time. It seems a shame to give up, but…"

"What would you say," asked Gus, "to combine the idea of a men's shed with a place where you could hand on some of your skills to the next generation?"

"I'm not sure what you mean," Archie said. "I'm not sure that I walked my garage invaded by a crowd of teenagers."

"I wasn't thinking of your garage. I realise the problem is finding a space that warm enough and big enough, but, supposing that was available, how would you feel?"

They discussed the idea and thought that it could work. Where could they find such a space?

"Let's see what we can do about this," Gus said. He had, he said, been impressed by their workmanship. They had done a great deal of the work using only hand tools, and they had begun with the basic materials, especially raw wood. Most new boatbuilding used not would but materials such as fibreglass. It will be wonderful to pass on some of the traditional skills.

I learned of this much later. The Community Centre Committee had to listen sympathetically to Gus's idea. It took several months of negotiation with the planners and the builders, but eventually it began to take shape. An extension was built on the back of the West Wing. Gus provided the money. It was a properly equipped workshop, out of the wind and rain, with access to the main part of the Centre, so that anybody working there could use the facilities, including the little café. The now Famous Four would act as instructors, welcoming youngsters from the age of fifteen. Their half -finished boat arrived a week after the Centre had been officially opened.

But that was still to come. As the Cymbeline was settled into her moorings once more, work on the Harbour Lights was under way. I was, of course, eager to look, but the entrance to the East Wing was already taped off. The great, stone flags which had formed the floors of the East Wing were being lifted and moved to make a great pile on the piece of land in front of the South Wing. They would be used, I understood, to form a patio. It was very heavy, laborious work. The flagstones were thicker and heavier than modern day paving stones. In some ways I had thought it was sad – we were camping on history. At least we were going to reuse the material. I could not get close enough to see more.

I left Elsie to her work, packed a bag, and tore myself away. It was not easy. I spent a week back at the

Pilgrims Rest. Nothing had changed since I left it nearly four years previously. The same peace and quiet, the same, well -manicured lawns, the same good but unadventurous cuisine, the same relaxed residents. I had changed, this hotel had not. I no longer belonged. I was trying to make myself relax, I had been told by my doctor that I needed to do this, to relax more, to step back from the stresses and strains of not only running but also building a modern hotel. I knew he was right, but following his advice was virtually impossible. I walked back to visit my old Kingfisher friend. I had no way of knowing if it was the same bird, but it might well have been. Certainly, the scenery had not changed.

One week later I returned to Goosemere and to Elsie. I was just in time to see her unload her kiln. That was an interesting experience, too. It was only the first firing. She was now faced with glazing all the contents and firing them again. My presence was not going to be welcome for long. I could not resist one more peek at the building, but work was still in progress on removing the flagstones. The Community Centre, on the other hand, was coming along more quickly now. The main, structural changes were nearing completion. The façade – the front of the Wing facing the cobbles – was now a complete wall with entrances at either end. Inside, there were the usual cloakrooms, a small café, an equally small area with seats, but the main part of the building was occupied by a large hall. This was not yet complete, but Elsie had explained to me that it would be equipped with movable partitions so that it could be used to accommodate smaller groups when necessary. Other rooms were also being prepared.

As I walked away, I was telling myself not to be so impatient. I was unable to do anything, and I did not like it. I was of no use to Elsie. I needed to occupy myself in some way, take my mind off the building. I decided as a first move to visit Tony and Megan, and my niece. I did not want to be a nuisance. The new baby, another girl, was still only a few months old.

"No, Tom, you would be very welcome!" It was Megan. I was fond of Megan. She was what was often called a motherly type. She loved children, but she was also a very warm hostess. "You won't be any trouble," she said, "really. You are house – or should I say hotel – trained. It is always difficult to get you to stop working. You nearly always forget that you are a guest. Please come. If I remember, you are also not a bad cook and that could be a blessing. Yes, as soon as you like, tomorrow?"

I stayed with them three weeks in all. I tried to pull my weight by doing the washing up or, rather, by loading the dishwasher, and by cooking a few meals, but I think it was pleasant for Megan especially and for Charlotte, my niece, to have someone to talk to. Tony was busy at school much of the time.

I could not stop myself: I drove back to Goosemere and, without stopping, drove straight down to check on progress. The area to the south of the South Wing now had a big pile of flagstones. At the junction of the South and East wings a trench had been dug, a trench which I realised was for the foundations of the new tower which would house the staircase and lifts. I have not fully appreciated how big it would be. Where the foundations met the original walls, they would have to be taken down. I had seen the plans, of course, but I wondered if I would approve of the changes. Then I shook my head, annoyed with myself. It was too late to worry about it. It would be far better if I could simply walk away altogether and return when it was all done. But I could not do that, I was far too involved.

Elsie had completed the second firing, and her small shop and studio were both now packed with goods for sale. She had several trade fairs booked. In the next four weeks we spent only occasional nights together. I did not accompany her. I would have been less of a help than a hindrance, as she put it. I spent a little time chatting to Gus. I tried to read to pass the time. Perhaps it was the conversations I'd had with Gus that made me think how much I had missed by leaving school so young. With time on my hands, maybe I should try to remedy my lack of knowledge. I visited the library for inspiration, then it struck me that I had already stumbled across a good starting point. The brief cruise on the Cymbeline had introduced me to Thames barges. I could spend a few weeks at least trying to learn a little more about local history, beginning with the river Gann. I had, after all, on that very first trip on the Moorhen, glimpsed the remains of the substantial wharves. What kind of trade did they do? What vessels visited the river? When did it all end? Yes, this was a good way to start. The librarian was extremely helpful. I left her with six books on my first visit. As I read my way through them, I visited the places they mentioned and took photographs, some of which I was able to compare with the original pictures. I began to learn a great deal about the commerce that took place until well into the 19th century. The coming of railways, the construction of bigger ships, and eventually the growth of roads had all contributed to the decline in trade. To maintain a navigable channel as far as the wharf would entail more and more dredging and that would have been extremely expensive. Thus, from a busy little port, Goosemere had shrunk to a small town.

Discovering more about Goosemere led me further afield. We were not far from the ancient city of Colchester. I began reading about that, too. I knew the Romans had settled there. (I also learned that British towns that ended in 'Chester' had all been garrison towns, and that 'Chester' came from the Roman word 'castra', meaning a military camp or garrison.) I mentioned some of this to Tony, half expecting him to treat my ignorance with scorn, but he did not do so. I began to realise why he was a teacher: he enjoyed seeing children learn and grow. I began to appreciate him more.

I continued to visit the Harbour Lights frequently. I remained impatient. At times it seemed there was nothing happening, but the time came when the steel frame which was to form the most important, structural element of the new tower, rose up. I had expected it to stop at the level of the original roof. After all, the buildings on either side were three stories high, but I have not allowed for the headgear of the lifts. That in effect added a further 8 feet. It was housed in a glass room. This would be accessible by stairs from the second floor and would provide a spectacular place in which to view the country all round. To the north and west this would encompass the old town and much of the new, allowing a glimpse of the Agronomy Station. To the south you would be able to look over the river towards salt marshes which continued to the East. The riverside buildings in the older part of the town gave way to more salt marsh and the claim of reflected light on the distant sea. I began to think this might be an attraction not only for guests, but also for other visitors to the town. I felt a little less anxious about the cost of the lifts.

"Tom, is your passport up to date?" Elsie asked one evening.

"I'm not sure, I think so. Why?" I was both puzzled and mildly alarmed.

"Can you find it?"

It was easy enough to find. I travelled light.

"Yes, it's still valid for another two years."

"Good. You are totally obsessed with this building," she said. "It's not good for you. Ever since you had those panic attacks, I have been worried. You certainly aren't doing what the doctor ordered."

"Of course, I am. I don't drink more than one cup of coffee a day these days, I hardly ever drink spirits. In fact, I don't drink very much alcohol. I take lots of exercise, I'm always walking up and down this hill."

"You know what I'm talking about," she said. "You were told not to work so hard."

"I'm not working at all these days. Chance would be a fine thing."

"Tom! You know very well what I mean. You spent far too much time worrying. I hate to think how many times a day you go and stare at a building site. There's nothing you can do about it. You have a site manager, and it is all under control. You just can't leave it alone and it is not good for you. The only thing for it, I've decided, is to take you away from it, a long way away."

"What are you saying?"

"Kitty is in Pembrokeshire still, isn't she?"

"Yes, you know she is. She liked it so much there that she is helping Colin's parents on their farm while Colin is in the Cotswolds."

"Right, I'm going to follow her example."

"I can't see you working on a farm," I joked.

"Maybe not. But then, I couldn't see you working on a ship, and that little trip was very successful."

"Elsie, I hate to think what you've got up your sleeve now. Have you got me a job as a steward on a liner or something?"

She laughed. "No. Seriously, though, there's nothing to keep you here until the hotel is finished. I imagine you'd like to be here with me when they finish the Community Centre. That won't be for at least six weeks, I'm told. So, taking a leaf out of Kitty's book, I'm going to introduce you to my parents."

This was a surprise. "Do they know about this?" I asked

"Oh yes, and they very much want to meet you."

"When are you thinking of?"

"I booked us flights on Thursday."

"This Thursday?"

"Unless you have an urgent operation in mind, why not?"

I was being swept off my feet. It might be fun. On the other hand, it might be quite daunting. I have no idea what to expect. Elsie had not talked much about her parents. They had retired quite early to live in Spain, that was about all I knew. She and they phoned every Sunday. I usually who left her to it, if I happened to be with her at that time. I have never spoken to them myself. I asked her what they were like. Her answers were evasive, general, remarks like "very relaxed" or "I'm sure you'll like them".

Part of me was still left in Goosemere as the plane took off, but I was sitting next to Elsie and that was good enough. At LC's suggestion I took with me a box of English breakfast tea. "They love English tea," she said. I was quite nervous as we walked to where the people were waiting. Elsie made a beeline for a couple in the front row, gave each of them a big hug and a kiss and then turned to me.

"This is Tom," she said, "my partner."

Her father was a good looking, bronzed man. He looked extremely fit. He was looking at me sternly.

"Partner in what sense?" he asked, "Business partner, or are you sleeping together?"

I was nonplussed.

"Oh, Daddy!" Elsie said, and her father laughed.

"Don't worry," he said," you will just have to get used to my sense of humour. We know a lot more about you than you probably do about us. We know that you and Louise have been together for some time now. She obviously loves you. I trust you love her. We trust her judgement. Now, let's get you home."

Her mother was equally welcoming. She was also equally fit. They were, they told me, living the life of Reilly. Over the next few weeks, I was to discover why they were so fit. They swam every day, they went riding two or three times a week, and they had a boat. They seldom stayed indoors, though, when they did, they ate splendid meals. The most pleasant thing about our relationship was that they treated us as equals. It was obvious how fond of their daughter they were and how happy she was to spend time with them, yet I was never to feel in any sense an intruder. I was very much part of the family.

Elsie's plan and had been to distract me. It was successful, and that was in large part down to the breathless lifestyle. I was not asked if I wanted to join them in all their activities; it was taken for granted. I was not able to refuse and, once I got used to it – it took about three days – I thoroughly enjoyed so much physical activity. Talk was largely trivial. There was, it seemed, nothing that anybody could worry about. Out of politeness they asked about our own lives in Goosemere, a town they still remembered, of course, but which they had no desire to return to. They made one concession: they would attend the Ground Opening of the Community Centre. That, they conceded, would be interesting, allowing them to see the changes in the town. I thought it tactful not to suggest they repeat their journey for the opening of the Harbour Lights.

Chapter nine

Before the plane touched down at Stanstead, Elsie said I was like a dog straining at the leash. I was anxious to see what had happened while we had been away. We came back when we did, not because the hotel was near completion, but because the Community Centre was almost complete. Elsie was eager to see the building, but she was also anxious to prepare for the Grand Opening. She had already negotiated by email and by telephone with people who would be involved, while Kitty had been busy advertising. Her website was impressive and alluring.

Almost as soon as we landed, I drove down to the Harbour Lights. I gave the Centre little more than a cursory glance, but noted It was looking splendid. The façade was now fresh and bright with a neat, clear sign, "Goosemere Community Centre" and all the woodwork had been painted. I did not bother to look much further, because my interest was on the other side of the cobbles. Much of the construction work on the East Wing had been done. Our project manager, Cyril Banks, met me at the door.

"There is still a lot to finish off," he said, "and it will look very different when the fittings and carpets are in place. Don't expect too much yet. The immediate change you will see will be to the floors, which are now smooth and level. You may not have noticed that the doorways are all a few inches wider to allow for wheelchair access. Otherwise, you may find the new layout confusing. I know you've seen the plans, but it's different when you see it in 3D."

He was right. The bare cements gave a cold impression which would change, once the floor covering was in place. Inside the familiar entrance, a door on the left led to the staircase, and one on the right opened into the bar. The bar wase smaller and it took a moment to understand that the wall at the back had been moved. That was to allow a passageway to be built between the kitchen and the new dining room. Cyril took me past the staircase to this corridor and so to the dining room. It was as yet simply an empty space without character. Guests would normally enter from the other side, where a door allowed access from the new, glass-fronted entrance. Here, even though the walls were still not finished and the floor was cement, I was taken aback. Light flooded in. This extension to the original building was encased in glass and it rose to the full height of the tower. At each level there were fire doors which gave way to the residential rooms. The lift, I was told, was not yet functional, but I climbed the stairs to the very top, to the level which housed the gear for the lift. This was secured behind metal doors in the centre, and around it was a viewing platform. Metal railings inside the glass allowed a spectator to stand safely and look at the landscape. I did just that.

There had already been substantial changes. The river frontage had been improved bya promenade. The old shed which had housed the Sailing Club, had gone. The open promenade provided better access to the Cymbeline, and railings along the river provided some security. No one would ever be able to run directly onto the mud as I had. Beyond the Cymbeline the promenade continued as a narrow, paved footpath for a further hundred yards, where it ended in a wooden hut, the hide where people could sit and watch birds.

I moved to the side of the tower which overlooked the South Wing. From here I could see that a terrace had been built along the south front, using the paving slabs that had once formed the floors of both the East and South Wings. It would be a pleasant place to sit in the sun. I could just make out over the roof that a similar use had been made of the slabs from the West Wing, providing a slightly smaller terrace on that side too. But what almost took my breath away was the view beyond the immediate buildings. Between the river and the Agronomy Station, its glasshouses glittering on the horizon in the low sunlight, there had once been a large, sloping field. It was now almost completely built over with new housing. I had not been prepared for such a rapid development. The small town had become very much bigger.

We went down and into the South Wing. The building was far from complete here, but the rooms had been rearranged. Somehow, it had proved possible to provide five, double rooms on each of the two upper floors, each with its own bathroom and shower. The fittings had not yet been installed, but I could see how they would end up. On the ground floor, space had been given to a lounge, and double doors gave onto the new terrace. There would also be toilets and washrooms at the end near the tower. I walked back to Elsie's tiny flat with a spring in my step.

Both Elsie and Kitty were so busy with the final arrangements for their Grand Opening that they paid little attention to what was going on in the hotel area. They did not need help from me. The Committee would have been running around like headless chickens, but for the sensible control exercised by the two women, the Chairwoman, and by Gus. Once more, the publicity drive involved a leaflet drop but this time there were many more houses. It would be interesting to discover how many of the new residents turned up. To encourage them there were some obvious attractions: the opening ceremony would be conducted by the Mayor in the new Hall. There would be one or two speeches, and several dignitaries. These included representatives of the council committee which had been responsible for approving the grant funding. The local TV station was sending a small crew. Refreshments would be available. Bunting and balloons would festoon the front of the building. In the smaller rooms several of the smaller groups had been invited to give demonstrations and they would be encouraged to sign up members of the public. The Famous Four, with help from Gus, would be installed in their Men's Shed, complete with boat. The Comprehensive School was supplying a small band. They were based at the school, but they had declared their intention to recruit members from the community who were interested in setting up other musical groups to work in the Centre. For those for whom the hustle, bustle and noise were too much, the new terrace on the western side was set out with tables and benches. Visitors would be able to sit and take in the view, though this was restricted. There was a small space between the edge of the terrace and a thin hedge which marked the beginning of the new, public car park. The car park had been introduced as part of the development plan, not specifically for the Community Centre, but it would serve a dual purpose and a footpath led round the south boundary to the new tower.

On the morning of the opening the Committee members and a group of willing volunteers swept the cobbles clean and ensured that the new Centre was spotless, windows gleaming. Work on the hotel was paused, but I was prepared for a few people to look round if they so wished.

The Opening was scheduled for 11 am. The first visitors began to arrive soon after 10, many of them on foot. Fortunately, it was a fine day. Fortunately, too, the Committee had made sure that the tea and coffee stall was already in place and operating. By 11 o'clock the courtyard was swarming with people of all ages. The smaller groups that were to demonstrate their skills had been allowed in, but the main Hall was still not open. The musicians were not wanted until after the speeches. The presence of a camera crew caused a lot of excitement.

The official visitors arrived by car at 10:50 on the dot. They were introduced to the committee one by one and then, using a large pair of shears, a ribbon across the main door to the Hall was cut and everybody made their way inside. I took a seat at the back. This kind of ceremony was intrinsically dull, but I felt something of the excitement and pleasure which Elsie, Kitty, Gus and the Committee must be feeling. This was, after all, a considerable achievement, the fruit of much hard work. Above all, as one of the speakers pointed out, it reflected well on the spirit of all those who had contributed either in cash or by the sweat of their brows. If the future programme were to be successful, the new Centre would make a real difference to the town and to many hundreds of people who lived there. Speeches over, the band took its place on the stage and launched into a programme of popular music. They proved to be very good. They were clearly popular and that gave me an idea.

After a while, I returned my empty teacup and took myself off to the hotel. By now I was getting familiar with the innovations, and I was impatient to complete the refurbishment. I had asked Kitty to help choose colour schemes but, when she suggested we should employ an interior designer, I realised she was right. By now, I was trying to stop worrying about the cost. Everything, amazingly, had been done within budget, but it was the kind of budget which made me wince. We could not spoil the ship for a ha'pennoth of tar. The designer was a lady called Hayley and she had firm ideas. She sketched her ideas for me. They were in light colours and shades, compensating in part for the old windows which were not exactly huge. The floors were a problem in that regard: they were to take a great deal of wear and it would not be practical if they were carpeted in such a way that they could not be kept clean. She compensated by using a great deal of lighting. She even had lights to illuminate the treads of the stairs. But I was particularly impressed by her designs for the bedrooms. . These walls were also ligh.t The rooms hinted at opulence, yet were not overcrowded nor fussy. Hayley and Kitty spent many, happy hours choosing such items as towels and bed linen and, something I had not thought of, suitable uniforms for the staff.

I say that I tried not to worry about money. Of course, I did worry. I was constantly taking note of all the small items which I had forgotten about or not even thought of at all. I resorted to my former habit of repeatedly checking spreadsheets. I concealed my anxiety, but on the numerous occasions that Elsie was not around in the evening, I sat for hours sometimes, feeling dejected.

Kitty was happy with all that was going on, she seemed happier than I had ever known her. Her stay with Colin's parents on their farm had given her lots of exercise and clean, Welsh air. It was not until the Centre had been running for nearly three weeks that I noticed there seemed to be a marked change in her. I mentioned it to Elsie.

"You've only just noticed?" she said.

"What exactly am I supposed to notice?"

"Don't you think," she asked, "Kitty is looking a little – well – plump?"

Light dawned. "Pregnant? Kitty? Surely not."

"Why not? She and Colin seem to be in a permanent relationship. If they want children, and I'm sure Kitty would want children, it makes sense not to wait too long. How old is she?"

"She's just over thirty. Are you sure?"

"She's your sister. I'm sure she will tell you in due course."

But it was only when I made clumsy hints that Kitty confirmed it. I told Elsie. It did not come as a surprise.

"How do you feel about children?" I asked. "At the moment we are the odd ones out. Tony has two daughters. Soon it looks as though my sister will be a mother. I have never thought about becoming a father."

"Perhaps we should talk about this," Elsie said. "We aren't compelled to have children, you know. I like children but I'm not really the motherly kind. I rather fancy they would limit our lifestyle and I'm not sure I want that. I am perfectly happy to be an aunt. I don't mind babysitting, but I don't think I want to have children myself. Is that a terrible disappointment?"

I thought for a while. "I don't think so," I said. "Like you, now I think about it, becoming a parent is a massive change in your life. I just might change my mind when I think about it more, but now I am happy with just you. I don't think I would like to share you. Perhaps it was not a good idea to bring this up."

"Tom," she said, "of course you were right to bring it up. Neither of us knew what the other thought and this is very important thing to decide. If you wanted children and I didn't, you might regret it in years to come. And vice versa, of course."

None of us had religious views. The fact that Colin and Kitty shared a bed, just as Elsie and I did, seemed a normal, healthy, and sensible arrangement. Marriage, I concluded, was more like a business contract. It offered a few, minor tax advantages and might possibly help with both financial and legal arrangements in old age, but merely to state publicly what we had both told each other, that we were fully committed to a lifelong partnership, seemed a work of supererogation. Most weddings, it seemed to me, were simply extravagant parties. Many, if not most of them these days took place not only after the partnership had been formed, but in many cases after children had been born. So, no children for us, we would be happy with our lives which were already full and rich. All the same, if Kitty wanted a wedding at some time in the future, it would be nice to be able to host it in the Harbour Lights.

There were unexpected consequences to the opening of the Community Centre. We had expected an initial surge of interest from the local residents. But I had not expected the publicity to be quite so effective. The small television crew which had covered the event drew the attention not only of the locals, but also of a small, independent television company. They were locally based and had local knowledge. They smelled a story, the story of how Goosemere had changed rapidly and on a large-scale. In effect, it was almost a new town. The old town still had its charm. There were several small shops and businesses to attract visitors, but the new development now offered a new primary school and a new venue for the surgery, much more modern, and a new library. There were yet only half a dozen small shops, but they included an excellent pharmacy. When the TV company began filming a documentary, they had to include the Agronomy Station. Most of us were ignorant about agronomy, so it was an interesting segment of the broadcast. It also brought home to me personally, who had met some of the agronomists when they had first stayed in the South Wing, how skilled these people were and how important their work, particularly in distant and developing parts of the world. The film makers moved from the Agronomy Station to the Community Centre, touching on some of the activities, and pointing out how they were to benefit the community. Since the camera had only to turn ninety degrees, it was a natural progression to mention the new hotel. It was as yet unfinished, but the very fact that it was mentioned, and the shots taken from the top of the new tower allowed a panoramic view, was very powerful publicity for us. The broadcast did not take place until several weeks after we had opened the hotel, but the filmmakers themselves attracted a great deal of attention. It was all good publicity.

The new Centre was a resounding success. Within a matter of days rooms and spaces were booked. Small clubs and societies came to light which had been meeting in private homes for the most part. They were largely handicrafts. They included such things as quilting, dressmaking, basket making, model making, including model trains, even a group which made greetings cards. Such groups only required small rooms to meet in, rooms which existed, though some were on the upper floor. The Committee was already beginning to think how to fund a small lift for the disabled. In the large hall there were various physical activities such as yoga and tai chi. The school band which had performed at the opening and had advertised for young people especially, had recruited more than a dozen. These were interested in a variety of musical skills and instruments, including the inevitable guitars, at least one drummer, two would-be clarinettists. It was an odd group. The enthusiastic music teacher from the school volunteered two hours a week to weld this strange group into shape. Once a week the noise coming from the Centre was, to put it politely, extraordinary.

One of the projects which featured in the original planning of the Centre was a repeat of the Open Mike evening, first staged in the old bar. The Committee could afford to be selective, inviting the more successful performers only. One of them, a young girl with a lovely voice, who wrote and performed her own songs, had become quite well known locally. She was booked for gigs in several pubs within a twenty-mile radius. Later she would be offered a contract by a London producer. As well as solo artists that evening featured several small groups. The standard was uneven, but generally enjoyable.

Four months after the opening of the Community Centre, we were ready to launch the hotel. Colin, Kitty and I had given this a great deal of thought. Our future and the future of the company we now formed depended on a successful beginning. We decided we had to spend money on the promotion. We invited the local MP to perform the opening ceremony. All guests would be invited to enter by way of the new foyer. They would be invited to inspect the new bedrooms and, in small numbers, to check out the view from the top of the tower. They could look into the kitchen, but they would be unable to spend time there, because a welcoming meal was being cooked. The inspection completed, they were invited into the new dining room. This was a bright, modern place. The gleaming white napery was almost the only, traditional touch. On the walls were paintings of ships, including sailing barges. We hired additional waiters and waitresses for the occasion. The chef with whom Colin had spent several months in the Cotswolds was happy to come along and help prepare a truly sumptuous meal. The guest list was carefully compiled. Naturally, it included those people who had been most helpful in our endeavour. John accepted the invitation. Roland thanked us but refused, saying he was busy. Tony, Megan and their two children enjoyed a family party which included a now heavily pregnant Kitty. Colin was busy in the kitchen, though he came in to accept the applause of the diners. Elsie and I sat at the same table. I had invited the Famous Four. At first they refused, saying it was 'too posh for them', but I persuaded them. Gus, too, was invited, as were many of the local businessmen and businesswomen. Several agronomists who had once stumped daily through the South Wing, now came in smart suits. The room was at capacity. The film maker was invited on her own, not as part of a team. A reporter from the local newspaper also attended, together with a professional photographer.

I had insisted on one small change when the new lobby and South Wing were being completed. I asked for a large display cabinet to be built on the wall leading into the South Wing lounge. It was to be glass fronted and consisted of several rows of squares, display spaces, approximately 18 inches square. Elsie provided figurines to fill the spaces, some of which had been languishing in her shop for months, some for years. At my request she had more recently produced half a dozen new ones. These were not the humorous models, but exquisite studies of geese, the large birds which gave the town its name. I loved them and we agreed they must be priced at £250. Both of us would rather keep them than sell them for less. Elsie did not have space to show the older models in her shop, nor did she feel she could sell them too cheaply. Each of them was a true work of art and had taken many hours. I suggested that her time was worth a minimum of £20 for each hour, but she pointed out that each figurine had taken at least twelve hours to create. No one, she said, was going to pay £240 for one of her figurines. We compromised. She agreed to display the older ones for sale at half that price, but she did not imagine she would sell any of them. Once in place, their bright colours behind the glass, made a wonderful display.

To our delight, within a few days of opening we received our first guests, six Japanese visitors who had come primarily to see the Agronomy Station. They were delightful guests, appreciative of the accommodation and especially the food. We were even more delighted when one of them asked if he could inspect one of Elsie's geese. I took the key and unlocked the cabinet. He inspected it minutely, turning it over to check the signature on the base. It was a very tactile piece and I watched with pleasure as he felt obliged to stroke the great wing feathers. I waited, expecting him to hand it back to me. Instead, he said he would like to buy it. I pointed to the small price tag which was discreetly displayed inside the pigeonhole. He merely nodded and asked if it could be carefully packed. When two more guests followed suit, I had great pleasure in passing on the news to Elsie.

"Oh dear," she said, "I shall have to do a lot more work."

The comic figurines proved quite popular with some of our other guests.

There was to be a steady stream of visitors to the Agronomy Station. They paid the full price for the rooms without a murmur. I had appointed one of our cleaners Housekeeper and insisted that every room should be meticulously cleaned every day. To ensure that this was so, for the first week I double checked every room. Indeed, I double checked every part of the hotel every day. This was the kind of work I was used to, but it was several years now since I had been so fully engaged in the day-to-day running of the place. I did not expect Colin to undertake much of the administration other than to ensure the kitchen was properly stocked. He was also generally in charge of the fish and chip shop which was now reopened and once more doing well. I occupied my new office whenever I could find a spare half hour, and my old habit of inspecting the figures two or three times a day meant that I had very little time to myself. By midnight most days I was exhausted, but I still felt obliged to be on duty most days by 7 o'clock in the morning. I did not realise how exhausting this routine was.

One evening I had been forced to deal with a small group of noisy teenagers who had spent the evening in the Community Centre and decided to buy chips before they went home to bed. They were being unnecessarily raucous. At first, they laughed when I asked them to quieten down, but eventually they did, throwing the packing from their chips on the ground as they made off towards the new houses. I was too weary to pick it up. I left it for the following morning and walked back to the door just as Elsie arrived from her workshop. I stopped for a moment, then found myself gasping for breath as a terrible pain caught me unawares in my left shoulder and arm. Within a second it gripped my chest as though in an enormous vice. I could not breathe, I could not speak, I could not move except to crumple slowly to the cobbles just outside the door.

I remember very little of what happened next. It is all, mercifully, confused. I found I was lying on my back on a bed of some sort. My chest still hurt. I could hear people speaking to me and over me, but I did not understand what they were saying. I have a vague impression of lying in an ambulance, of a male nurse, of wires and bleeping noises and just out of focus, the anxious face of Elsie. I did not regain full consciousness until the following day.

I was in hospital.

"Well," said a man who was presumably a doctor, "it's good to see you come back to us."

I had no idea what he meant.

"You have had a serious heart attack," he explained. "We shall keep you in for observation for a few days. Your partner here," he waved a hand to where Elsie stood, "tells us that you have been working far too hard recently. You owe her an enormous debt of gratitude. She was with you when you collapsed. If it wasn't for her quick thinking and expertise, I don't think you would be here today."

"Thank you," I croaked, but my voice sounded strange even to me.

I discovered the full truth over the next few days. When I collapsed, Elsie had rolled me on my back and realised I was no longer breathing. Without hesitation, she checked my airways and began CPR, pausing just long enough to shout for help. Colin heard her and called for an ambulance, but it took twenty minutes to arrive. Between them they continued CPR. That, I realised, explained why my back was so painful from the cobbles. It also explained why I had a bad bruise in the middle of my chest, where Elsie's hand had pressed down so heavily on my breastbone. After three days I was released and driven home. I walked shakily through the new entrance, feeling thoroughly grateful for the lift which took me to our bedroom. As I took the few paces to the lift, I was touched to find six of the staff applauding me. Kitty and Colin were tempted to fuss, but Elsie told them tactfully that I needed to rest. She helped me get into bed where I felt so weak, I was close to tears.

When Elsie said that she was not maternal by nature, her understanding of the word was that it meant softly feminine. I did not need that kind of love. I needed honesty. Elsie had always been honest with me rather than sentimental. Now she insisted on a regime which was dictated by the doctor. She knew I would worry about the hotel if she simply kept all information away from me, so she kept me informed, but she ensured that her reports were positive. Any problems, however minor, she kept to herself. Kitty, although pregnant, was able to deal with the finances, but she and Colin agreed the only way to keep the business running smoothly was to employ a hotel manager. I can't remember how they described the appointment to me. I'm sure they did not tell me they were appointing a new, hotel manager. That would have upset me very badly at the time. They probably said that they were hiring some administrative help. They interviewed five candidates and asked Elsie to help them. Between them they had been obliged to write a full description of the duties involved. As they did so, they realise that I had been obsessive in my concern that everything ran smoothly, that several of the key staff were perfectly capable of managing their own section of the hotel, that I did not need and had never needed to duplicate their efforts. I had been found out: my old failing, the inability to delegate, had taken its toll. Now I had no choice.

Part of my recovery involved taking regular exercise. I resumed my habit of walking along the promenade and the new footpath to the top of the hill as far as the farm gate. Here I would rest and lean back against the gate. The view to my left was now populated with new houses. The roofs of the Harbour Lights were largely unchanged, except for the new tower, its glass reflecting light like a beacon. Where in the past the road from the old town had forked, there was now a traffic roundabout, and even the riverbank had changed with the addition of safety railings. It was different but not unpleasant.

Now, when I made my way back down the hill, Gus would sometimes hail me and invite me on board for a cup of tea. I was not allowed to drink coffee or alcohol. I had never thanked Gus for what he had done for the Four. His gesture, paying for the extension of the building to create a purpose-built Men's Shed, had given them and you sense of purpose. They were enthusiastic about finishing their boat. But they were also enjoying the companionship of the young boys and young men who were learning the basic skills of long ago. Some of the boat building skills which might have died out were now being saved. Everybody was a winner.

"Do you think," I asked him, "they will actually finish their boat, or is it all just an excuse to carry on?"

"Oh yes, they will certainly finish it. And it is really very good little boat. All the people working on it, youngsters, and all, will be really proud of it. We might even persuade you to come out fishing in it one day."

I did not reply to this.

"Do you reckon that the Centre is proving to be the success everybody hoped for?" I asked.

"Yes, that's for sure. Of course, once the initial enthusiasm has died down a bit, it may require effort, and there will be jobs that no one wants to take on, like looking after the bookings. Your sister is doing that now. She's a bit like you. She doesn't know when to stop, but, once the baby is born, she won't have so much time. "

Ernest, the new Manager, was hard-working and efficient. There was no need for Elsie to report any problems because he had nearly always solved them. Eventually, Kitty broke the news to me that he was appointed as Hotel Manager. Surprisingly, I was not terribly upset. I was, after all, still one of three Directors. However, one evening Elsie found me sitting in my new office in silence, computer switched off.

"Hello," she said. "You look – well, not so much bored as grumpy."

"Are you surprised? After several years' hard work, I am now part owner of a hotel which seems to be successful. My fellow directors have kindly appointed a Hotel Manager and I have nothing to do. I'm fed up with being idle."

"Oh dear! I'm sorry you feel like that. You are still under doctor's orders, don't forget. But I do understand. I'd feel the same way. The fact is that everything is well under control and it's going well. We are beginning to make money. You don't have to lift a finger."

"I should be more grateful, I suppose."

"Tom," she said, suddenly serious, "you can't have any idea how I felt when you had your heart attack. I thought I'd lost you. "

"Have I ever thanked you?"

"Probably. Does it matter?"

"Yes, of course it matters, especially when you make a habit of saving my life. I still think about that horrible moment when I was drowning in the mud, or about to, and you crawled out along that ladder."

"Well, all's well that ends well. I just don't want you to do it again. By that I mean I don't want to have to save you the third time. In the words of the song I've got you under my skin."

I stood up and we held each other close for a few minutes.

"Tom," she said, "why don't you get away for a few days or weeks? It might distract you, stop you wanting to be busy in the hotel."

We talked a little longer. Kitty's baby was not due for another four weeks. I rang Tony. He and Megan would be delighted to see me, as would Charlotte. "You can get into practice of dealing with a baby," he said.

I had been told not to drive, so I took the train. Even that felt unnecessarily lazy, although I had gone back to reading a great deal. Elsie's geese had awakened my interest in wildfowl. Before, I thought a goose was a domesticated bird. They all looked the same to me. I remembered the Romans had used them as watchdogs. More than that I knew nothing. Now I discovered just how many kinds of geese there were. I also learned of their migrations. I had not realised that Goosemere and the wetlands around it were staging posts for the migration of geese from as far afield as Russia. The green plants which I had noticed at the beginning in the field beyond the farm gate, were sugar beet. I now learned that local farmers were in the habit of leaving their nutritious leaves for the geese to feed on. By the time I had read the three books I talk with me, I was beginning to be an expert. (My expertise was severely challenged on my return by Elsie: her knowledge was of a far greater range of wildfowl then just geese.)

Megan was quite right about looking after children in general. Charlotte was not yet of school age and she and I got on well, relieving some of the pressure on her mother. On two or three occasions she and I took a bus from Tony's school gates and went exploring together. The days passed quickly and enjoyably without strain. I took my medicine and my exercise and grew steadily stronger. It was a hugely enjoyable interviewed.

There was one, exceptional day, and that was the day on which I visited my father, now in his last year in prison. Perhaps it was a mistake. I came away depressed. I had no idea that he intended to leave the country immediately his probation began. No doubt, with his usual contempt for authority, he had a good idea that his absence would not be noticed for two weeks. Two years later I was to receive a letter with a Venezuelan stamp, telling me that he was safe and sound and doing well. There was no address.

I returned to the Harbour Lights after three weeks. Everyone was pleased to see me, they said, but they were all busy running the business. Kitty suggested we might have a Board Meeting, but I suggested in my turn that it would be wise to wait until after the baby was born. I suggested to her that one little job I might undertake was the bookings for the Community Centre. She had a very well organised computer program which worked rather like a spreadsheet, that is, by typing in a booking for a particular venue, it automatically adjusted any parts of the system that were affected. It was relatively simple to use. Since the bookings were coming in, thick and fast, I felt I was doing something useful at last. Ernest continued to do a good job. He was polite enough to ask my opinion sometimes, but I had little to offer.

It was nearly a year later that Elsie and I repeated our trip on the Moorhen. I promised her I would not have a heart attack on condition she did not expect me to go skinny dipping. Neither of us caught any fish, and we returned to the new landing stage without getting muddy. We stood on the wooden platform and embraced. I was happy, although things had not turned out as I had planned or expected.

Kitty gave birth to a boy, Kevin, causing jubilation. I grew used to the sound of a baby crying and found it surprisingly agreeable. It made me feel I was near the centre of the family, almost for the first time in my life.

Kevin was nearly a year old when I got Elsie to drive four of us back to visit our mother's grave. It was the fourth anniversary of her death. We arranged for Tony, Megan, Charlotte and Helen to meet us there. So, it was a family party that found Its way across the small churchyard, eight of us with two pushchairs between us. When we approached the grave, Kitty stopped suddenly.

"Is that a new headstone?" she asked.

"Yes," I said, "I had to get permission from the vicar. I felt we needed to do this."

The headstone was quite simple, a plain piece of granite. The inscription was equally simple, it read, "Rosemary Hammond, 1050-2015, remembered by her children, Kitty, Tony, Tom and sister, Emily."

Both Tony and Kitty stared at me.

"I'm so glad," Kitty said. "Most of all because you included your own name."

"In many ways," I said, "she had a poor life and not really all that long. 65 is quite young these days." We stood for a few moments and laid the flowers on the grave until the children began to get restless.

There are many kinds of love. I don't know if forgiveness is one of them. I can't even be sure that I forgave my mother. I certainly accepted her for what she was. Nearly 40 years previously she had carried me, maybe even looked forward to my birth, only to suffer extreme physical pain followed by mental anguish. I knew I was not personally responsible. Possibly, if you could think of it all rationally, she knew that herself, but by some tragic quirk of psychology, we had both been crippled for decades. She had found some consolation in her two other children, but it had taken me nearly 40 years to recover.

I was silent for most of the journey home. I was thankful to have emerged from an extraordinary period. When my father had first taken me to view the ruinous Harbour Lights, I was a solitary young man. I had no friends to speak of, I was not even emotionally close to my siblings, certainly not to either of my parents. I had colleagues and I had subordinates. I had a single aim, one day to become hotel manager of a large establishment. In the few years since then I had made some real friends who not only helped and supported me, but who also gave me people to care for. I had come to terms with the treatment my mother had given me, and my father was no longer part of my life. Yet it had been his intervention which had changed me. I was now closer to both Tony and Kitty than I had ever been. As for Elsie and me, our relationship was honest, open, and more satisfying than anything I had ever known before. My single-minded ambition had somehow faded. I didn't think of myself as the owner of the Harbour Lights, but as part of a team that looked after it. Elsie's clever plan to persuade me to sell part of the buildings, had given me an unexpected source of pleasure by cementing my relationship with the community. I contributed more to the running of the Centre than to the hotel, now managed by Ernest

In the back of the car the children were asleep. I shot a quick glance at Elsie, who was driving. She noticed and smiled. I settled back in the passenger seat and closed my eyes.

THE END

Lightning Source UK Ltd.
Milton Keynes UK
UKHW040624201222
414205UK00002B/430